The Case of the
Worried Waitress

Erle Stanley Gardner

BALLANTINE BOOKS • NEW YORK

ISBN 0-345-33193-1

This edition published by arrangement with William Morrow and Company, Inc.

Manufactured in the United States of America

First Ballantine Books Edition: June 1986

Foreword

My longtime friend, Marshall Houts, editor of the highly technical publication, *Trauma*, which is put out by Matthew Bender & Company, is an expert in the field of legal medicine.

Marshall Houts has had a varied career. He was for years an F.B.I. Agent, then he did confidential work for the Government in foreign countries, after which he started practicing law in Minnesota.

Houts became interested in the Court of Last Resort, and gave up a lucrative law practice in order to become an investigator for the Court of Last Resort, making considerable financial sacrifices in order to promote the cause of justice. He investigated several murder cases in which innocent men had been wrongfully convicted and brought those cases to a satisfactory conclusion. Watching his work, I acquired a profound respect for the man's ability and integrity.

Then Houts originated the idea of a publication dealing with trauma in the field of legal medicine, and for years has been putting out this publication for Matthew Bender & Company.

Some time ago, Marshall Houts wrote me about Don Harper Mills, M.D., LL.B., who practices forensic medicine in Los Angeles.

I have received permission from Marshall Houts to quote from his letter and I am including the quote here as a Foreword because I think it covers the field admirably.

Houts said in his letter:

> Most people think of the field of legal and forensic medicine as being primarily limited to the practice of criminal law and the administration of criminal justice. This is because the men in this field who attain publicity usually do so because they have investigated a spectacular murder case which makes the headlines.
>
> In actuality, forensic medicine has a far wider application in the field of civil litigation than it does in the criminal field. Both the American Medical Association and the American Bar Association estimate that between 75 and 80 percent of the cases that reach the courtroom today turn, in some degree, on a question involving medicine. For example, the passenger in an automobile

who ends up with a "frozen shoulder" must have his legal case evaluated by competent doctors and lawyers who are well versed in the field of medicine, to determine whether his bad shoulder was actually caused by the automobile accident, and what the nature and extent of his disability is. In the final analysis, skilled doctors and lawyers in the medico-legal field must arrive at a difficult decision as to just what his injury is worth in dollars and cents, so that the defendant who caused it, or his insurance company, can be forced to pay damages.

Don Mills represents a new type of medico-legal or forensic medical specialist who combines both a medical degree and a law degree in an effort to render a valuable service in cases involving compensable injury.

Don Mills' work includes the evaluation and the actual trial of all types of personal injury actions. Some of these are medical malpractice suits against doctors; some involve head injuries that arise from automobile accidents; some involve slipped or ruptured intervertebral discs which result from the so-called whiplash type of injury; some involve injuries that are sustained at work and which are covered by the Workmen's Compensation laws, etc., etc., etc.

I have never met Don's father, but for a great number of years he was considered the leading authority in the United States on environmental medicine. As a result, he was invited by various governments of foreign countries to investigate the climate of a given country and assess its effect on the people.

I think the above comments by Marshall Houts are just about as comprehensive as one could ask for.

Too few people understand the growing importance of the field of legal medicine. Many doctors fail to realize the extent to which legal medicine has become important during the past decade.

And because I know Marshall Houts so well, and know that his enthusiastic endorsement of Dr. Mills means that the doctor is an outstanding figure in the field of legal medicine, I am dedicating this book to

DON HARPER MILLS, M.D., LL.B.

ERLE STANLEY GARDNER

Cast of Characters

Chapter 1

Perry Mason and Della Street were having lunch at Madison's Midtown Milestone.

Mason had just started to say something to his secretary when he noticed a shadow across the table and looked up to see the smiling eyes of Kelsey Madison, the proprietor.

"How is everything, Mr. Mason?" Madison asked.

"Fine," Mason said. "The food is up to your usual standard."

"How's the service?"

"Wonderful!"

Madison glanced quickly over his shoulder, then lowered his voice. "I mean that latter, Perry. How's the service?"

Mason seemed mildly surprised. "Perfect!"

"The reason I asked," Madison said, "is that I've just found out the waitress who is waiting on you bought you from another waitress."

"What do you mean?" Mason asked.

"You may have noticed," Madison said, "that the girl who brought you your butter, water, knives and forks, and handed you the menus was not the same girl who returned to take the order."

"I hadn't noticed that," Mason said. "As a matter of fact, Della and I were somewhat preoccupied."

"So I noticed," Madison said, "and I disliked to intrude, but we don't encourage buying tables."

"Just what do you mean by that?" Mason asked.

"It's a custom in some of the restaurants," Madison said. "The head waitress will assign a waitress to a table. If the diner happens to be a customer that is considered a liberal tipper, some other waitress may want to buy the table.

"For instance, if a man is a twenty percent tipper and his bill is going to come to five dollars or more—which means an almost certain dollar tip—one waitress will offer to buy the table for perhaps as much as fifty cents.

"The waitress who sells the table pockets the fifty cents, has a chance to rest her feet a bit. The girl who has bought the table takes on the extra work but makes fifty cents profit. It just depends on how much the girls happen to want money."

"And I'm supposed to be a big tipper?" Mason asked.

"You quite frequently are, Perry. If a girl gives you good service, you'll tip up to twenty-five percent—sometimes more. But somehow I have an idea Kit was interested in something beside the tip, and that's where I come in."

"What do you mean?"

"If she should try to get some legal advice from you, I'd appreciate knowing about it. You know how it is with doctors and lawyers. They are constantly being beset by people who want special service without paying for it."

"Give it no thought," Mason said.

"It's just the fact that Kit is new here and I wanted to see what she had in mind."

"Kit?" Mason asked.

"Katherine Ellis. They call her 'Kit,' or sometimes 'Kitten.' She hasn't been here very long and she's not a thoroughly professional waitress. This is her first job as waitress."

"Well, thanks for the warning," Mason said.

"It's more than a warning, Perry. If she tries to get anything out of you, will you let me know?"

Mason regarded the restaurant man speculatively for a few seconds, then suddenly smiled. "No," he said.

"No?"

"No," Mason said. "I am not an informer. I appreciate the warning, and forewarned is forearmed; but if you want to find out if Kit is trying to get professional information from your customers, you're going to have to get someone else to tell you."

"Okay," Madison said, "but I'll be watching from the sidelines. Here she comes now with your order."

Madison moved casually away, without seeming to devote the least attention to the young waitress who brought two corned beef sandwiches, a glass of milk and a cup of coffee.

She put the dishes down in front of Mason and Della Street. "Cream and sugar in the coffee?" she asked Della.

Della Street shook her head. "I'm taking it black."

The waitress set the carton containing the milk and the glass in front of Mason, stood there for a moment looking the table over. "Is there anything else?" she asked.

"I think that's it," Mason said.

Again she hesitated.

Della Street flashed a meaning glance at Mason and looked back toward the kitchen where Madison was standing with his arms folded, apparently surveying the entire dining room, but actually keeping a close watch on the waitress.

"Everything's fine," Mason said.

"Thank you," Kit muttered and turned away.

Mason turned to Della Street. "What do you say, Della?"

"Very definitely," Della said. "She has something on her mind, but she doesn't quite know how to make the approach."

"Or else she was aware that Madison was standing back there giving her the eagle eye," Mason said.

The lawyer passed the jar of special mustard to Della, then helped himself—spreading the condiment liberally over the corned beef.

"Got one of my cards handy?" Mason asked.

Della Street nodded, reached into her handbag, brought out her purse, extracted a card. "Why?" she asked.

Mason grinned and said, "I'm just following a hunch. Pass me the card under the table."

The lawyer surreptitiously wrote on the card: "My usual fee for an office consultation is ten dollars. The tip under the plate is eleven dollars."

The lawyer slipped a ten-dollar bill and one dollar bill unobtrusively from his pocket and placed the eleven dollars and the card under the oval-shaped platter on which the sandwich had been served.

Della Street watched him with amusement.

"Suppose," she asked, "this isn't what the girl had in mind? Suppose she just wants an autograph?"

"In that case," Mason said, "she has an autograph and the Bar Association will probably be in a position to accuse me of soliciting business."

They laughed, went ahead with their lunch, finished their sandwiches, and almost instantly Kit was at the table. "Is there anything else?" she asked.

"That's all," Mason said.

Kit stood there apparently scribbling on a check which Mason noticed had already been made out.

"Would it be possible to ask you a question, Mr. Mason?" she asked.

"Yes," Mason told her, "at my office," and scraping back his chair, reached for Della's chair.

His smile was disarming.

Kit's face fell. "Oh," she said, and handed him the check.

"The tip," Mason said, "is under the plate."

"Thank *you!*" the girl responded icily.

Mason took Della Street's elbow and piloted her toward the cashier's cage.

Della Street looked back over her shoulder.

"Mad?" Mason asked.

"Rebuffed," Della Street said. "Oh, oh! Now she's looked under the plate!"

"Reaction?" Mason asked.

"Can't tell," Della Street said. "She has her back to us now."

"Well," Mason said, "if Kelsey Madison was watching to see if one of his waitresses was trying to get free legal opinions, he can relax now. What was her name, Della?"

"Katherine Ellis," Della said. "I've made a note of it."

"If she comes to the office, let me know," Mason said.

"You'll see her?" Della Street asked.

"Any time," Mason said. "And charge her ten dollars for the visit."

Chapter 2

It was shortly after ten o'clock the next morning when Della Street relayed a phone call from the receptionist in the outer office and said, "Miss Ellis is here, Perry."

"Ellis?" Mason asked, groping momentarily in his memory.

"Kit Ellis, the waitress."

"Oh," Mason said and smiled. "Bring her in, Della."

Della went to the outer office and a few moments later returned with a radiant Kit Ellis in tow.

"Mr. Mason, I don't know how I can ever thank you! You're *so* understanding."

Mason smiled. "I trust the tip was adequate?" he asked.

Kit Ellis produced the ten dollars, handed it to Della Street and said, "I'm paying your secretary right now for a consultation. I can't begin to tell you how much I appreciate the way you handled it. I'm afraid that Mr. Madison thought I was going to impose on you and . . . Well, it's wonderful of you to handle it this way."

Mason said, "Sit down, Miss Ellis, and tell me what's bothering you."

She said, "It's my Aunt Sophia."

"What about her?" Mason asked.

"She's a mystery."

"Many women are," Mason said. "But I take it in this case, since you want to consult an attorney, you have some cause for alarm?"

"Not for alarm exactly," she said, "but for worry."

"Perhaps you'd better outline the facts."

She said, "I'm twenty-two years old. We lived back East. My parents were both killed in an automobile accident six months ago. I had only seen my aunt once when I was a little girl, but I made it a point to write to her twice a

5

month—nice newsy letters about what I was doing and all of that."

"And what were you doing?" Mason asked.

"Attending school mostly. My father made a lot of money and, as it turned out, was spending all he made. I had always wanted to be a lawyer and he wanted me to have a legal education. I was taking a pre-legal course at the university at the time of his death.

"Not only was his death a great shock but, when it came to finances, I was in for a still greater shock.

"It seems that Dad had a perfectly enormous income judged by ordinary standards, but it was the type of income that was cut off instantaneously upon his death. The house had a first mortgage, a second trust deed; the new cars were being purchased on credit, and installments were due on everything in the house. That was the way Dad lived—easy come, easy go! He was a real estate salesman and he could literally talk the birds out of the trees. But he not only spent his commissions as fast as he'd get them, he borrowed on commissions as soon as the deals were in escrow. . . . Well, anyway, when I examined the accounts I found I was penniless."

"Your mother hadn't salted anything away?" Mason asked.

She shook her head. "Mother just worshiped the ground Dad walked on. She let him make all the decisions and felt that he couldn't be wrong. And I guess that's right. The only thing he was wrong on was life insurance. He didn't believe in that. He believed in living and letting live, was the way he expressed it.

"Anyway, that's all more or less beside the point, Mr. Mason."

"The point, I take it, is," Mason said, "that your Aunt Sophia asked you to come and stay with her and you decided to accept."

Kit Ellis nodded.

"Why?" Mason asked. "Since it was quite evident you were going to have to go to work, I would have thought that you would have much preferred to have stayed in your

6

home town, arranged to share an apartment with one or two women of your own age and . . ."

She shook her head and said by way of interruption, "I just couldn't face my friends, Mr. Mason. Dad had always been most generous with me. I'd had an allowance of my own, a car of my own, I had no financial worries, I was usually the hostess when girls in my sorority went out, and . . . Well, I just couldn't bear the thought of such an abrupt change and . . . These things probably will seem minor within a couple of years but, right at the moment, they were the biggest problems in my life; and they certainly loomed large.

"Above all, I didn't want people to feel sorry for me. I couldn't bear the thought of waiting tables, for instance, and having some of my sorority sisters smile sweetly at me and leave me a too generous tip because they were sorry for me."

"Why wait tables?" Mason asked.

"Because," she said, "it was all I could do. I tried to get a job. If I could have waited longer, I could have probably been able to get a fair job; but I had absolutely no experience—not only in working, but in applying for a job. I'm afraid I said the wrong things at the wrong times.

"Anyhow, Aunt Sophia asked me to come out here and live with her, at least for a while. She was lonely and had a house with two spare bedrooms and said she'd be glad to have me living with her."

"So you came out here?" Mason asked.

Kit Ellis nodded.

"And did you intend to go to work when you came out?"

"No, I didn't. We had always thought that Aunt Sophia was well fixed. At one time she was, but she had her own tragedy and apparently her own financial disaster."

"Go ahead," Mason said, his voice showing his interest. "Tell me what happened."

"Well, I got out here and moved in with Aunt Sophia and thought that perhaps I could continue my college studies—either working my way through college or perhaps getting a job for a year and saving money and . . . Well, let's not be hypocritical, Mr. Mason. I thought perhaps Aunt Sophia would suggest that she would pick up the tab for going ahead with my education."

"She didn't?" Mason asked.

"She didn't. Instead, she . . . I hardly know how to tell it."

"Did you," Mason asked, "want to see me about your aunt?"

"In a way, yes."

"What about her?"

"It's a long story," she said, "and it's a difficult story to tell, but I'll give you the highlights. My aunt was my father's sister. She was a career woman. We all thought she was pretty well fixed, and I guess she was. She had this house and property that I generally considered was rather adequate.

"Gerald Atwood came into her life about two years ago, and I guess, if you want to look at it that way, it was a scandal.

"Atwood was married to Bernice but had separated from her. Bernice was one of those bitchy women, if you'll pardon the expression; cold-blooded and possessive, and a typical example of the statement that hell hath no fury like a woman scorned.

"When Atwood and his wife separated he gave her money to go to Nevada and get a divorce. Then Gerald met Sophia and wanted to marry her. He asked Bernice for the divorce papers. Bernice kept stalling, so finally Gerald and Aunt Sophia went to Mexico and reported that they had been married, but actually if there ever was any ceremony it wasn't worth the paper it was written on.

"I guess Gerald Atwood was a big plunger. He and Bernice had lived in Palm Springs, and since he had an office in his house there, he kept the house and spent a lot of time there. It was about the only piece of property he hadn't deeded to Bernice.

"Gerald went over to Palm Springs one weekend to straighten up some things. He expected to be there for a few days. It was rather late in the season and beginning to get warm. He went out to play golf, became overheated and died on the course.

8

"The old card records at the club showed that Bernice was his wife. Since she was living there in Palm Springs, the golf course found her telephone listing and notified her of Gerald's death.

"Bernice did a very thorough job. She went down to the golf course and took immediate charge of the body. She made funeral arrangements, then she took the keys to the Palm Springs house, moved in there and apparently just ransacked everything.

"Aunt Sophia didn't know anything about Gerald's death until she became alarmed when he didn't phone her, telephoned the house and Bernice answered the telephone. Bernice told her she was in charge, that she had made the funeral arrangements, and suggested that in the interests of the proprieties Sophia should not try to attend the funeral."

"Hadn't there been any divorce really?" Mason asked.

"Apparently not. Bernice had told him she was getting a divorce in Nevada, but apparently she hadn't even filed the papers."

"No property settlement?" Mason asked.

"Oh, sure, there was a property settlement, but it was all oral. You see, Bernice had just about everything in her own name, and she just kept it and left Gerald stripped of his property. He was planning to start over again.

"Aunt Sophia said to forget the property, that she'd give him a stake to get started again. Then she evidently cashed in just about everything she had and turned the money over to Gerald."

"Can she get any of it back?" Mason asked.

"Apparently not—not now that Gerald is dead and Bernice is his widow. Aunt Sophia turned the money over to Gerald as an outright gift. He made the investments entirely in his own name, and Aunt Sophia becomes vague whenever one talks about a marriage.

"You see that at the time they were supposed to have been married, I *think* Gerald had begun to suspect that Bernice hadn't really filed for divorce in Nevada. Therefore, any marriage they might have made would have been a bigamous marriage and Bernice could have had him arrested for that. So Gerald didn't want to be vulnerable on that point.

"I think that he and Aunt Sophia just took a trip down to Mexico and came back and told friends they'd been married in Mexico, and everyone took the statement at its face value. But Aunt Sophia gets very, very vague whenever I ask about the Mexican marriage. She has confessed to me that it probably wasn't any good anyway. I don't think there ever *was* any Mexican marriage."

"In such circumstances," Mason said, "it's sometimes possible to show a joint venture in the nature of a partnership, and your aunt would be entitled to half of the property that Gerald had at the time of his death. It's a tricky bit of legal business and depends entirely on how the money was turned over, whether it was an outright gift, whether it was deposited as part of a joint venture, or how it was handled. Do you know anything about the financial end of the case?"

"Not a thing," she said, "except what I've told you, and Aunt Sophia refuses to have anything to do with Bernice. She says that Bernice can keep her money, that money doesn't mean happiness, that Bernice is just a greedy, cold-blooded, money-grabbing parasite and that if she wants money bad enough she can keep the whole thing."

"But that leaves your aunt wiped out?"

"That's what I wanted to talk to you about, Mr. Mason. One of the things."

"Go ahead," Mason invited.

"I discovered, after coming here and talking with my aunt, that she had turned all her ready cash over to Gerald Atwood, and his death had left her pretty well wiped out. Aunt Sophia didn't say anything about sending me back to college for a law degree—which was what I wanted—and I didn't say anything.

"Then things began to happen and . . . well, frankly, Mr. Mason, I don't want to live in that house any longer than I have to, and in order to get out, I have to have a job and be independent."

"What things happened?" Mason asked.

"Mysterious things," she said. "Things that bother me and—things that frighten me."

"Go on," Mason invited.

"Aunt Sophia is one of the most penurious women I know—in certain respects."

"In her dealings with you?" Mason asked.

"In her dealings with me and in her dealings with others. I have a room, a place to stay; I have board, and that's it. I couldn't carry on my work in college because I have no transportation, no clothes except the ones I brought with me. In other words, without some outside help, continuing with college was impossible."

"Go on," Mason said.

"Well, I started out with the feeling that Aunt Sophia was fairly well off. The house certainly is spacious and comfortable. She has a gardener to take care of the outside, and she gets around to do the housekeeping herself. She won't have a housekeeper in the place—says they don't do an hour's real work in half a day."

"So you started helping out with the housekeeping?" Mason asked.

"Kit nodded.

"And then?" Mason asked.

"Then," she said; "I almost starved to death."

"How come?"

"Aunt Sophia would take the papers and study the ads for the specials at the big food markets. If she could save three cents on a pound of butter at one store, five cents on a pound of bacon at another, she'd go from one to the other, buying just the specials that were advertised for that day.

"And the food she served at the table was just about enough to keep a bird alive. I was terribly hungry most of the time."

"So you decided to go to work?" Mason asked.

"I decided to go to work and that would give me an excuse to have my lunches out, so I could at least have one good meal a day."

"Go on," Mason said.

"I encountered the same trouble here that I'd had back

11

East. I had a classical education, but I had absolutely no experience."

"Most girls lie about their experience in order to get their first job," Mason said, watching her closely.

"I don't lie, Mr. Mason."

"You told prospective employers the literal truth?"

She nodded.

"Go ahead," Mason said.

"I told them the truth and I didn't get to first base. I told them I was willing to learn on the job, but I needed enough for bus fare, for lunch money, for routine expenses—and by the time a girl keeps herself well-groomed with her hair, her stockings, her clothes, shoes—well, it takes money."

Mason nodded.

"So," she said, "I wound up getting a job as a waitress at Madison's place and mighty glad to get it.

"I don't know all the tricks of the trade yet. I don't know how to get a big tip out of the average customer, but I try to do a good job, and I let people know I'm trying. And, of course, one nice thing is that I get my meals. In fact, I can gorge myself if I want, and believe me I wanted for the first few days. I just never was so hungry in my life."

"Madison is satisfied with your work?" Mason asked.

"Heavens, I don't know that he knows that I'm alive, but the headwaiter who runs the dining room is all right. I have a horrible feeling that sooner or later he's going to make a pass and that my job may depend on things I don't like to think about, but right now everything's okay."

"Those are occupational hazards," Mason said, his eyes twinkling, "that an attorney can't do much about. Why did you come to me, Miss Ellis?"

"Actually," she said, "it was on the spur of the moment. When you and Miss Street came into the restaurant yesterday and one of the girls pointed you out as the famous attorney, I . . . Well, I bought you. I gave the waitress who had your table seventy-five cents for the privilege of taking over."

"What did you have in mind?"

"I don't kow what I had in mind, but I do know that somebody squealed to Mr. Madison, and he started watching me like a hawk. I guess waitresses are not supposed to bother customers with personal problems, and one can very readily see the reason for that."

Mason nodded.

"But," she said, "you were intuitive and so perfectly wonderful, I don't know how I can ever thank you."

"That's all right," Mason said, "but I'm interested in the reason back of all this."

"The reason back of this is that Aunt Sophia is some kind of a high-powered fraud and is living a lie, and it bothers me."

"Yes?" Mason prompted.

"She goes from one food market to another picking up the special that's been advertised in the paper, saving a few cents on her daily grocery bill, but the point is she goes from one food mart to another by taxicab, has the driver wait while she's shopping. Her cab bill must be simply enormous."

Mason's eyes glinted with sudden interest. "Aside from that she seems normal?" he asked.

"No, she doesn't," Kit said. "She has a closet in her bedroom and the top shelf has a row of hatboxes. She keeps the door of that closet locked and . . . I feel terrible about this, Mr. Mason."

Mason smiled. "You mean your curiosity was aroused and you wanted to see what was inside of that closet?"

"After I found out about the taxicabs," she said, "I became terribly curious about the closet. There's a spring lock on there and she always keeps it locked.

"Well, remember I help with the housework. A couple of mornings ago when I went in to clean her bedroom while she was out, I found the closet door unlocked."

"So you peeked in?"

"I didn't peek. I went right inside with the portable vacuum cleaner. That part of it was all right, but there was a whole stack of hatboxes on the shelf and I wondered why Aunt Sophia would have all that collection of hats.

"That's where my feminine curiosity got the better of me, and I opened the box on the end to see what the hat looked like.

"The hat was full of money."

"How much money?"

"I don't know—a lot. The bills were in fifties and hundreds."

"What about the other boxes?"

"I don't know. I put the lid back on the box I'd opened and got out of there, and when I did I closed the door and the spring lock snapped shut.

"Now, then, Mr. Mason, that's what bothers me. There may be a fortune in money in that house, and if burglars should find out about it—well, two women living alone that way . . . And then I'm worried about Aunt Sophia. You know what happens when a person starts saving money like that. It usually means they're cheating on the income tax, and if Aunt Sophia is well fixed and has been building up a supply of money on which she has been paying no tax, something will be done about it sooner or later."

"With an elderly woman," Mason said, "I think the authorities would make an allowance. Many elderly people are . . ."

"But she's not like that. She's not elderly. She's only fifty-five and she's a very attractive fifty-five at that. To see her face you'd think she was in her forties, but she dresses old."

"How did you find out about the taxicabs?" Mason asked.

"I was at one of the food stores, because when she'd been reading the ad in the paper about a special sale on bacon, I had seen something in the appliance department that I had wanted, so I got off my bus and was just ready to enter the store when a taxicab drove up and out stepped Aunt Sophia, apparently telling the drive to wait."

"So what did you do?"

"I faded into the background and waited. Aunt Sophia was gone a good ten minutes and then she came out with a single package, presumably a pound of bacon. She put that in the taxicab and drove off. The cab went sufficiently close to me so that I could see that there were other packages in there on the seat."

"She doesn't use the taxicab to go and come?" Mason asked.

"Heavens, no, she leaves on the bus and she comes back on the bus with a shopping bag filled with her bargains."

"Is this all that caused you to want to talk with me?"

She said, "Mr. Mason, I want your advice. I don't want Aunt Sophia to think I'm running out on her, but I don't think I should stay there in that house under all the circumstances."

"Why would your aunt feel that you were running out on her, Katherine?" Mason asked.

"Well, she's facing things all alone. My father was her brother. He was the only living relative, aside from me. I'm all that she has left. She's had severe tragedies in her life. I feel sorry for her."

"What happened to the Palm Springs house?" Mason asked abruptly.

"Bernice is living in it. She applied for letters of administration as the surviving widow."

"There was no will?"

"Of course, there was a will," Katherine Ellis said. "It was in the office in the Palm Springs house, and Bernice got her hands on it and burned it."

"Gerald Atwood left no other relatives?"

"No. Bernice has a son by a prior marriage, Hubert Deering. There are no other children, no relatives, and Bernice is just determined to take the whole thing. She swears the property, which actually was acquired by Gerald Atwood with money that Sophia gave him to invest, is community property."

"Has Sophia contested Bernice's claim?"

"Sophia is keeping quiet like a little mouse," Katherine said, "and I don't like it. She acts as though she had an ace up her sleeve somewhere, but she's just going along living a drab life, saying nothing and living in that horrible two-and-a-half-story haunted house."

"Haunted?" Mason asked.

Katherine Ellis lowered her eyes. "I wasn't going to say anything about that."

"Haunted houses are a hobby of mine," Mason said, his

eyes showing his interest. "If the house is haunted, I'd like to know about it. What do you hear—moans, groans, squeaking steps at night, or . . ."

"Steps at night."

"What kind of steps?"

"Walking steps where a person simply could not be walking."

"Why not?"

"Climbing up and down stairs," Katherine Ellis said, "with sure steps walking through pitch-dark corridors, all without the faintest ray of light. Then sibilant whisperings; then more steps and . . ."

"Perhaps your Aunt Sophia has some clandestine visitor," Mason said.

"Not in the dead of night and in pitch-darkness. I've surreptitiously opened my door enough so I can see the place is in complete darkness."

Mason thought for a moment, then said, "Very frankly, Katherine, I don't like it. I don't like any part of the situation in which you find yourself. I think you had better get out."

"When?"

"Now," Mason said. "Get out while the getting's good."

"What will I tell Aunt Sophia? Will I tell her that I found out she was keeping a huge sum of money and . . ."

"Tell her nothing of the sort," Mason said. "Simply tell her that you've decided to get an apartment with a girl of your own age."

"But that will take time and it may require more money than I'm making. After all, we make the biggest part of our income from tips, and, believe me, getting a good tip from a customer is something of an art."

Mason said, "All that can come later, but I want you out of there now!"

"What do you mean 'now'?"

"What time do you go to work?"

"Today I go to work at eleven-thirty, work until three-thirty; then I'm off until five o'clock when I go on and work until nine."

16

"You don't go home just for the short time off in afternoon?"

"No, there's a sort of a rest room and lounge for the waitresses who are off duty, where we can have slant boards and put our feet up, take a shower, lie around and relax and take a nap on a sofa."

Mason said, "When you get off at nine o'clock, go home. Pack up your things. Get out."

"Where will I go? I can't . . ."

"Go to a motel. Get out of that house," Mason said. "It's dangerous. Not only is it dangerous because the money there may be tempting to outsiders, but if anything should happen to it, you would be the first prime suspect.

"Quite evidently your Aunt Sophia has been less than frank with you. She's been nice to you, you owe her a certain amount of loyalty, but I think you've discharged your obligation. Anyway, you have yourself to think of."

She said. "I was thinking about getting a detective to shadow Aunt Sophia and see where she goes and perhaps find out . . ."

Mason shook his head. "A detective would cost you fifty dollars a day and expenses. You can't afford it and you can't afford to have your Aunt Sophia ever find you were . . . No, get out! Telephone your aunt that you've decided to make other arrangements and that you're moving out tonight. I take it you don't have a great many personal belongings?"

"Very few. I left my house with virtually nothing except the clothes I had on and some simple travel outfits. I have two suitcases and a handbag. I deliberately cut everything down so that I could travel light. I have a couple of cartons of intimate family things coming by freight, and by the time they get here I can afford to pay for storage. I've made up my mind that I'm going to have to get accustomed to living without a lot of money and a lot of worldly possessions."

Mason said, "Get out of that house just as soon as you decently can. Leave a note with Miss Street here, giving her your aunt's name and address; and when you get located, presumably at a motel for the night, telephone and let us know where you are."

17

"I can reach you after office hours?"

Mason thought for a moment, then said, "You can reach me through the Drake Detective Agency. That's run by Paul Drake. That outfit does all my investigative work. They're in the building with us, on the same floor and . . ."

"Yes, I noticed the name on the door as I left the elevator. It was that that gave me the idea of trying to find out something about what really is back of Aunt Sophia's peculiar conduct."

"Forget it," Mason said. "You've given me your problem; you're going to follow my advice. Ring up your aunt, tell her you're going to move this evening, and then when you go back from work, have your things packed up, get a taxicab and go to a motel. What's the address where Aunt Sophia is living?"

Katherine Ellis took a card from her pocket and handed it to Mason. "I had these printed," she said, "when I was applying for jobs."

Mason studied the address. "There are some very good motels about half a mile or a mile farther down the boulevard, and I think your same bus line runs right on past them. But don't bother with a bus—you'll have baggage and it'll be night. Don't go standing around on the streets waiting for a bus. Get a taxicab. You have money enough for that?"

"Oh yes."

"What does your aunt look like?" Mason asked casually.

"She's five foot three; in her mid-fifties, but could pass for forty-five; medium size; good figure; steely gray eyes; chestnut hair; weight about a hundred and eighteen—a smart-looking woman if she wants to dress up, but she likes to dress old and talk old."

"All right," Mason said, "telephone and let me know when you get settled so I'll know where you are."

Chapter 3

When Katherine Ellis had left the office, Mason regarded Della Street quizzically. "Now then," he said, "why the devil should a woman study the newspapers to find where she can save three cents on a pound of butter or five cents on a pound of bacon, and then go shopping from one market to another using a taxicab and having the taxicab wait, at a cost of three or four dollars an hour, while she's making her bargain purchases? Then why should she have the taxicab deposit her at a bus line, wait for a bus and finish up the last lap of her journey on a bus?"

Della Street shook her head. "I don't get it," she said.

"It's quite obvious to me," Mason said, "that this Sophia Atwood is playing a rather deep game. Give Paul Drake a ring and ask him to come in."

"Chief," Della Street protested, "you aren't going to try to . . ."

"Yes, I am," Mason interposed. "Our client is mixed up in something deep and potentially dangerous. For all we know the whole scheme of having her come to live with Aunt Sophia may have been to get what the confidence men call a patsy, or a fall guy.

"One of the bad things about the administration of justice is that it takes money to make the wheels go around. Katherine Ellis doesn't have the money to do the things she needs for her own protection. We're going to do some of them for her.

"A lawyer has a duty to his clients. I can afford to hire a detective. Kit Ellis can't."

"Chief," Della Street charged, "you had all this in mind when you asked Katherine Ellis to describe her aunt in detail."

Mason grinned. "No use trying to keep secrets from a

secretary," he said. "All right, you read my mind. Tell Paul to come in."

Della rang the Drake Detective Agency, and a few moments later Paul Drake gave his code knock at the door of Mason's office.

Della let him in.

Drake said, "Hi, Perry. Hi, beautiful. What's the good word today? Got a job for me?"

"I've got a job," Mason said. "I want a job of tailing done and I don't want your operative to get caught even if he has to let the subject go."

"Who's the subject?"

"A Sophia Atwood," Mason said. "Here's her address."

He passed the card Katherine Ellis had given him over to Paul Drake.

"What is this—an apartment house?" Drake asked.

"A two-and-a-half-story private dwelling," Mason said. "Probably the house is pretty old and run-down and the lot is worth five times as much as the house."

"Description of the person I'm to shadow?"

"Fifty-odd, looks considerably younger in the face but dresses older. A neat figure; chestnut hair; five foot three; weighs about a hundred and eighteen; steely gray eyes.

"Now then, I'll give you a tip. She'll leave the house, walk to a bus line, take a bus—I don't know how far—then get off the bus, transfer to a taxicab, do a lot of shopping in a taxicab, have the cab drive her to the bus line, pay off the cab, take her purchases, climb aboard a crowded bus, travel several blocks, get off the bus and walk a block and a half to the house."

"Well, I'll be damned," Drake said.

"Exactly," Mason agreed.

"What's the object of doing all this?"

"That," Mason said, "is what I'd like to find out."

"Can you tell me anything about your client?"

"In this part of the job I haven't any client," Mason said. "I'm satisfying my curiosity and I don't want you running up any fancy bills on expenses. On the other hand, I do want a good competent tailing job done and I don't want the subject to have any idea that she's being followed."

"Okay," Drake said with a grin, "you came to the right place. You think the shenanigans will go on today?"

"I'm going to be out your per diem if they don't," Mason said.

"I take it you want immediate action."

"Starting as of now," Mason told him.

"Okay," Drake said. "I've got a good man I can put on it. He'll be on his way in a matter of minutes."

Chapter 4

It was after five o'clock when Paul Drake's code knock sounded on Mason's door.

Della Street opened the door and Mason said, "Hi, Paul. We're getting ready to call it a day, and it's been some day."

"Thought I'd catch you before you left," Drake said. "I've run into something that puzzles me."

"What's that?" Mason asked.

"This Sophia Atwood deal. My man uncovered something puzzling. He reported by telephone a short time ago, and I thought I'd better come in and tell you the story."

"Where was he phoning from?" Mason asked.

"Actually he was phoning from his car," Drake said. "We've got several cars with telephones in them and this man is using one. He telephoned from out in front of the two-and-a-half-story residence, but he was using the phone in his car."

"Okay," Mason said. "What's the pitch?"

"Guess what the aunt really does for a living?"

"You mean she works?"

"She works," Drake said.

"What does she do?"

"She sells pencils."

"Pencils?"

"That's right. She has an air cushion, a dark smock, some dark eyeglasses, a stock of pencils, and she's a fixture in front of the offices of the Gillco Manufacturing Company out on Alvareno Street."

"Goes there every day?" Mason asked.

"Off and on."

"Don't they object?"

"Apparently not. One of the big stockholders in the

company passed the word along the line that she wasn't to be disturbed."

"How much time does she put in selling pencils?" Mason asked.

"I can't get the whole sketch," Drake said. "My man didn't want to ask too many questions, but at times she'll be there darn near all day. Other times she'll show up for just an hour or two."

"How does she come and go?" Mason asked.

"Taxicab."

"Doesn't it arouse comment that a pencil peddler should arrive by taxicab?"

"It's the same cab all the time," Drake said, "and the story is that the cabdriver has some sort of arrangement on a monthly basis to drive her where she wants to go."

"Check on her marketing?" Mason asked.

"Yes, she goes from one market to another picking up specials. She goes by taxicab, and apparently this time it isn't the same cab every time. At least it's not the same cab that she uses when she's taken to her stand in front of the Gillco Manufacturing Company."

"What about the Gillco Manufacturing Company?"

"Electronics, gadgets, modern scientific stuff. It does manufacturing on its own and also acts as sole importing agent for one of the Japanese factories. It . . ."

The phone rang.

Della Street looking inquiringly at Mason.

The lawyer shrugged his shoulders, said, "Okay, Della, we'll take this one last call."

Della, now that the switchboard operator had gone home and her phone was connected directly with the switchboard, picked up the instrument and said, "Perry Mason's office . . . Yes, this is Miss Street . . . Who? . . . What is it about? . . . Oh, I see. Just a minute. I'll see if I can catch him. He's just leaving the office."

Della cupped her hand over the mouthpiece, said to Perry Mason, "It's your client, Kit Ellis, and she's in serious trouble. She wants to know if it's possible for you to get in touch with her right away."

Mason hesitated a moment, exchanged glances with Paul Drake, then said, "Okay, Della, I'll talk with her."

The lawyer picked up the phone on his desk.

"Mr. Mason," Kit said, "I know this is a terrible imposition, but it's almost a matter of life or death with me. Could you come out here?"

"Where is here?" Mason asked.

"Where I am living—Aunt Sophia's house. You have the address."

"What seems to be the trouble?"

"I am being accused of theft."

"By whom? By your aunt?"

"Not exactly. By some smart alec who says he's a 'friend of the family.' His name is Stuart Baxley. Someone should take this pompous . . ."

"Don't talk like that," Mason warned, his eyes narrowing.

"Well, Baxley is here, and he's urging Aunt Sophia to have me arrested; and there's a detective here and . . ."

"Have you said anything?" Mason asked.

"What do you mean, 'Have I said anything'? I told them they're crazy. I . . ."

"Have you said anything about any of the things you told me about?"

"Not so far, no."

Mason said, "Sit tight. Say you haven't stolen anything. Aside from that, say nothing to anyone about anything. Don't answer any questions except to state that your attorney is on his way out and your attorney will do all the talking. Do you understand?"

"Yes."

"I take it," Mason said, "that your aunt has suffered a pecuniary loss."

"Apparently."

"From the money that was hoarded?"

"Well, it's a long story and involved."

"Say nothing," Mason said. "Answer no questions. Say you are innocent of any crime but are referring everything to me. When I get there, follow my lead."

Mason slammed the telephone back in the cradle, nodded to Della Street. "Let's go, Della," he said. The lawyer made for the door, held it open, said to Paul Drake, "Keep on the job, Paul. I'll phone in to see what's new, but call off your shadow. His presence out there may attract attention now.

"Come on, Della."

Della grabbed her purse, snaked her coat off the hook. Mason held the coat for her and they strode down the corridor, Della Street's heels beating a rapid tattoo as she tried to keep up with Mason's longer steps. Drake came behind them at a more leisurely pace.

"Good heavens, Chief," Della said as Mason punched the elevator button, "if the aunt's lost all of the money in the hatboxes, it could be a fortune . . . and how much do we really know about our client?"

"Of course, we don't *know* what's in the hatboxes," Mason said. "We can only . . . ."

The cage came to a stop, the door slip open, and Mason piloted Della Street into the cage and motioned her to silence.

They hurried to the parking lot. Mason got his car out and drove skillfully through the streets, making time wherever he could until he came to the big two-and-a-half-story house on the upper side of the canyon drive.

The lawyer parked his car, helped Della out, and together they ran up the steps to the porch.

Mason rang the front doorbell and almost immediately it was opened by a broad-shouldered, belligerent individual, in his middle forties, who said brusquely, "You can't come in!"

Mason said, "Permit me to introduce myself. I'm Perry Mason, an attorney. I'm representing Katherine Ellis, who I believe is inside. This is Miss Street, my secretary. I want to see my client."

"You can't come in!"

"Who says so?"

"I say so," a voice announced, and the broad-shouldered man stepped aside to make way for a peppery man who stood barring the way and who seemed to be trying to take charge of the situation.

"I am Stuart Baxley," this man said. "I am a friend of the family. Sophia has been the victim of an atrocious, dastardly crime perpetrated by Katherine Ellis, and I propose to see that Miss Ellis pays for her misdeed.

"If you want to talk with your client, you may talk with her *after* she arrives at the police station."

"You have notified the police?" Mason asked.

"We're notifying them."

"You are the police?"

"Certainly not. I told you who I am."

Mason raised his voice. "Come on out, Katherine!" he shouted. "You're going with me."

"Indeed she is *not* going with you," Baxley said.

"You're going to restrain her?"

"Yes."

"By force?"

"If necessary. This gentleman behind me is a private detective, Mr. Levering Jordan of Moffatt and Jordan, Investigators. He is completing his investigation. When he completes it, we propose to make a formal arrest, either through the police or as a citizen's arrest."

Mason said, "I'm not going to try to force my way into your house or Sophia Atwood's house, but I *am* going to talk with my client."

Mason heard hurried steps, then Katherine Ellis in the background said, "Here I am, Mr. Mason."

Stuart Baxley turned and started toward her.

Mason raised his voice. "You lay a finger on my client, Baxley, and I'll break your neck! Come on, Katherine, you're going with us."

"You can't do this," Baxley said.

Levering Lordan said, "Take it easy, Mr. Baxley. Mr. Mason is a well-known attorney."

"Well, he can't break *anybody's* neck," Baxley said.

Mason grinned. "I can try."

"There are two of us," Baxley said to Jordan, "and *you're* a pretty husky individual."

"There are legal points involved," Jordan demurred.

Mason turned to face Katherine. "Come on, Katherine. Walk toward me. If anybody tries to detain you, try to break away from him and let me come to your assistance. Now, let's have the legal formalities straight, gentlemen. Is anyone making a citizen's arrest?"

"I'm making a citizen's arrest," Baxley said.

"Better take it easy, Mr. Baxley," Jordan warned.

"All right," Mason said, "you're a citizen. You've made an arrest. This is my client. Having arrested her, your duty now is to take her before the nearest and most accessible magistrate. I'll accompany you. Come on, Katherine."

"Now, wait a minute, wait a minute," Jordan said. "We still have a little investigative work to do. Miss Ellis has been very much of a problem."

"In what way?" Mason asked.

"She refuses to give us her fingerprints. I have pointed out that we can get those fingerprints as soon as she is booked at a police station."

"Come on, Katherine," Mason said. "What are you waiting for?"

Baxley made a move as though to block the exit, but Katherine Ellis slithered around him and made a run for the door.

Jordan made no effort to stop her.

"Dammit, Jordan," Baxley said, "get her! Grab her!"

Mason put his arm around Katherine's waist, passed her over to Della Street, then turned to face Baxley and Jordan.

"Miss Ellis is now in my custody," he said.

Baxley came blustering to the door. "Well, you're not going to take her away from here!"

"Want to bet?" Mason asked.

"Do something, Jordan. Dammit, do something," Baxley stormed.

"Mr. Jordan," Mason explained, "isn't feeling particularly lucky at the moment."

Jordan stepped back, said something in a low voice to Baxley.

Mason said, "Come on, Kit," turned and escorted Della Street and Katherine Ellis down to where his car was parked.

Katherine said, "I can't leave here, Mr. Mason. I haven't a thing out of my room—not even a toothbrush. I . . ."

"You're leaving," Mason said. "There are a lot more important things at stake than a toothbrush. I see you have your purse."

"Yes, I hung on to that through all of the melee."

"How much of a melee?"

"Verbal."

"And what did you say?"

"I said nothing except what you had told me to. I said that I had not taken any money, that I was not going to answer any questions except in the presence of my attorney because I was innocent of any crime and I felt that they didn't have any right to ask me questions. I repeated that over and over again."

"Good girl!" Mason said.

"She's trembling like a leaf in the wind," Della Street said, her arm around Katherine Ellis's shoulders.

"I know," Mason said. "We're going where we can talk."

"Where?" Katherine asked. "Your office?"

"That's too far," Mason said. "We're going down the road to the first good motel we find. We're going to register there, then we're going to see about getting your things. You're not working today, Katherine?"

"Not tonight. I told Mr. Madison I was going to move and he said to take the evening off so I could get settled."

"Okay, we'll go find a motel," Mason said. "I think there are some of them on the main boulevard on the other side of this canyon road."

Mason helped Della Street and Katherine Ellis into the front seat of his automobile, said, "We'll sit three in front. I'll drive and talk and I want you to listen."

He closed the door on the right side, walked around to the driver's seat, got in, started the car, and drove slowly into the stream of traffic.

"Now, Katherine," he said, "I may not have time to talk to you in detail because they may notify the police and a radio cruiser may pick us up.

"Any statement you make to me as your attorney or to Miss Street, or in the presence of Miss Street as my secretary, is confidential.

"Now, the reason I had to ask you to refuse to make any statement was that we—all three of us—know that you have been guilty of doing things you shouldn't. Your curiosity got the better of you. You went prowling into that closet where you had no right to be.

"The minute you touched that hatbox you made yourself

vulnerable. Now, how much does your aunt claim is missing?"

"A hundred dollars."

"What?" Mason asked in surprise.

"A hundred dollars."

"Out of that hatbox which was filled with money?"

"Mr. Mason, there's something funny. That hatbox isn't filled with money any more. The hatbox is empty."

"What about the other hatboxes that were on the shelf?"

"All gone."

"And faced with a loss of what may be several hundred thousand dollars, your Aunt Sophia claims that she's lost only a hundred?"

"Yes."

"Well, I'll be damned!" Mason muttered under his breath.

"Stuart Baxley came to call on her this afternoon. She invited him for dinner and she invited me for dinner. It looked as if she might be trying to play Cupid. She went up to her room and left us alone for ten or fifteen minutes. Then all of a sudden she started screaming that she had been robbed.

"Baxley ran upstairs to see what it was all about. I followed him at a more sedate pace.

"She was standing there at the door of her closet pointing to the empty shelf and repeating over and over, 'I've been robbed.'

"Finally Stuart got her calmed down and—well, you can imagine how *I* felt. *I* was in a panic."

Mason brought his car to a halt at a boulevard stop, said, "Go on."

"Stuart asked her how much she'd lost and she told him immediately that she had lost a hundred dollars; that she had put a hundred dollars in the hatbox this morning and that the hatbox was now empty."

"What did she say about the other hatboxes?"

"Nothing."

"And what did Baxley say?"

"Oh, good old Baxley!" Katherine Ellis exploded. "He's evidently resented me ever since I came there and, of course he was the first to insinuate that *I* had been home and had had an opportunity to get into the closet and take the money."

"How long had you been home?"

"I had the afternoon off and I put in a good part of it doing some personal shopping. Then I went home and packed. Aunt Sophia came and invited me for dinner. I accepted."

"Then what happened?"

"Then Aunt Sophia told me that Stuart Baxley was coming for dinner."

"You'd met him before?"

"Yes, rather briefly."

"Just what do you know about him?"

"Absolutely nothing."

"He says he's a friend of the family."

"Well, he isn't a friend of the family because there isn't any family. That is, there isn't now—not since my folks were killed in the auto smash. But I don't think my folks ever did know him. My dad just wasn't a letter writer, and Aunt Sophia was more or less a name to us.

"I would write Aunt Sophia every couple of weeks—newsy little letters telling her what was going on, because I didn't want her to feel alone. And she'd answer with brief letters, but always telling me how much she appreciated hearing from me and how much it meant to her; and then she'd go on writing about various little things—about music she'd heard on the radio that had impressed her. Actually she told me very little about herself, but even so, she never mentioned the name of Stuart Baxley."

"How much did you see of him?" Mason asked.

"Not very much. We had ten or fifteen minutes' conversation while Aunt Sophia was upstairs. He seemed rather evasive, I thought."

"Did he tell you what he did?"

"He said he did investments and a little financing now and then, and I thought he was trying to keep from giving me any very specific information about himself."

"You didn't ask him how long he'd know Aunt Sophia?"

"Oh no. I didn't ask any really personal questions. We

30

were sort of sparring around with a lot of small talk. He asked me how I liked it out here and said he understood I had taken a job. And I told him I had, and he wanted to know why, and I told him I had to support myself. He seemed to digest that information as something that was rather important. I don't know why."

"I think," Mason said thoughtfully, "we'll find out a little more about Stuart Baxley. You know there's just a possibility he could be some kind of snooper."

"What do you mean by that?"

Mason said, "He might have found out that your aunt presents a penurious front but has hidden assets. After all, a woman who drives up to market in a taxicab and keeps it waiting while she goes in to shop for the daily special is rather a vulnerable target for the people who like to capitalize on that sort of thing.

"There are people, you know, who give tips to the Internal Revenue and, if tax frauds are discovered as a result of those tips, they get a reward."

"Well," she said, "that's just the sort of man you'd think he was from the impression he makes. There's something furtive about him—something about the way he shrugs off all personal questions and then changes the subject.

"He did ask me how I liked Aunt Sophia's cooking, and I told him she was a wonderful cook but that I had been eating out since I had the job. I *think* he was trying to sound me out to find what kind of a table she set, but I gathered he had been there for dinner once before."

"Do you know if your aunt had planned anything special for dinner?"

"No, I don't. She came in on the bus with some shopping bags. She'd been to the market. I don't know what she had."

"What would she have ordinarily at dinner?"

"Things would be very, very skimpy. She'd get perhaps three frankfurters. She'd heat them up and give me two because I was a growing girl and needed nourishment. She'd take one for herself. Then she'd have bread and butter and some kind of canned vegetable, and that would be it. I've never been as hungry in my life as some of the nights I spent there in the house before I went out and got the job."

"All right," Mason said. "After your aunt discovered her loss and announced that she had been robbed, then what happened?"

"That was when Baxley started asking Aunt Sophia to call the police. And then when she said she didn't want police messing in her business, Baxley said he knew a private detective who could get fingerprints from the hatboxes."

"The boxes were gone?" Mason asked.

"All except one. There was one empty box on the floor."

"So then what?"

"Stuart called this detective agency, I heard the name. It was Moffatt and Jordan. I tried to get you and the line was busy. Then things started happening very rapidly. This man, Jordan, came out and he was very rough and abusive. He demanded that I give him my fingerprints and I wouldn't do it. I told him I was going to call you. Then they told me they were going to call the police, and I told them to go ahead; then I got you on the telephone and . . . . well, you know the rest."

Mason, who had been driving slowly and cautiously after he entered the main boulevard, turned in at the Wolverine Motel. He had Katherine Ellis sign the register, identified himself to the manager, and said, "Miss Ellis is a client of mine. This is my secretary, Della Street. We're going to be with Miss Ellis for a little while."

"Quite all right," the manager said. "I recognized you when you came in, Mr. Mason. It's a pleasure to be able to be of service in connection with any of your cases."

"Thank you," Mason said.

They went to the unit which had been assigned to Katherine Ellis, seated themselves somewhat awkwardly, and Mason said, "I have some news for you, Katherine. I've found out a little something about your aunt's background. However, I think it's best that you don't know just what I've found out—at least for a while.

"I think probably we'll be hearing more about this. I think police will enter the case sooner or later, and I think you'll be questioned. I don't want you to tell a lie. Therefore I think there are some things that it's better for you not to know.

32

"Now then, our vulnerable point is that you found the hatbox full of money. The minute you admit that to the police or to anybody else, they're going to jump to the conclusion that you stole a lot of money from your aunt; that your aunt had this money hidden away and is afraid to admit how much it was; therefore she says it was only a hundred dollars.

"The police won't be able to *prove* anything except by inference. But they'll elect you as the guilty party and let it go at that. They won't carry an investigation any further because they'll believe they have the case solved.

"Therefore I don't want you to tell anybody about what you found in that closet, and yet I don't want you to lie about it.

"That puts you in a very serious situation. You have to state that you aren't going to make *any* statement except through me and in my presence.

"Now that, of course, looks very suspicious; so I'm going to try to make it sound more logical by stating that you're a very sensitive young woman; you have had a very cultured background; that you are not accustomed to the seamy side of existence and that you have been accused of theft by Stuart Baxley and by this detective agency; that you're going to sue both of them for defamation of character; and the thing which is holding up the filing of the suit at the present time and the reason I don't want you to make any statement is that you don't know whether or not you are going to include your aunt as a defendant in that lawsuit; that until we have reached that decision, I have instructed you to make absolutely no statement to anyone."

She nodded.

"Think you can handle that all right?" Mason asked.

"Why, of course. I'm not unintelligent, Mr. Mason. After all, I've had quite a bit of education. I'll simply state that the matter is in your hands; that you're intending to file suit, but there are technical problems in connection with the suit and we don't know as yet whether my aunt will be a party; that I have been told to make no statement of any kind to anybody about anything until you tell me to."

"That's the girl!" Mason said.

Mason crossed over to the writing desk, found some stationery, said to Katherine Ellis, "Now, write a letter to Sophia Atwood. Tell her that I am your attorney; that you left because threats were being made; that you can be reached in care of me; that Della Street is authorized to go to your room and pack up your things and bring them to you; that, if she can't pack all of the things in one trip, she will return at a later date, but that you are urgently in need of things for tonight."

"Good heavens," Katherine said, "they'll throw you out. They won't let you . . ."

"They're not going to *throw* me out," Mason said. "They may keep us from getting in, but I don't think they will."

Katherine Ellis hesitated for a moment, then started scribbling on the paper. When she had finished, she handed the note to Perry Mason. "Is that satisfactory?" she asked.

Mason read the note carefully, then nodded. "Put a date on it," he said.

She dated it.

"You've had dinner?" Mason asked.

"No."

Mason handed her a twenty-dollar bill. "You're going to need some expense money," he said. "There's a restaurant here in the motel. Go and get yourself a dinner."

"I couldn't eat, Mr. Mason. I'm too upset. I feel all churned up inside."

"That's fine," Mason said. "That's a normal reaction. Just stretch out, try to get some rest, and try to calm your nerves. We'll be back, probably within an hour."

The lawyer got to his feet, nodded to Della Street, and they went out.

From the first telephone Mason called Paul Drake.

"There have been doings out at Sophia Atwood's house, Paul," Mason told the detective. "I may as well tell you right now that my client, Katherine Ellis, is being accused of taking money from a hatbox that was in an upstairs closet. Now then, I want some information."

"Shoot," Drake said.

"What do you know about Moffatt and Jordan, Investigators?"

34

"They're a reputable detective agency," Drake said. "They're a cut above the average in ability."

"Is Jordan skillful enough to get fingerprints from a hatbox, Paul?"

"I doubt it," Drake said. "You can't get fingerprints from paper—not without using iodine fumes, and even then you have to be lucky. But it takes laboratory conditions to do it."

Mason said, "I've got news for you, Paul. The Macdonell Associates of Corning, New York, have worked out a new technique by which a black magnetic dust is applied to a surface so gently that nothing except the dust actually touches the surface. Then the dust is removed magnetically, and the process is so ingenious that it leaves identifiable fingerprints on pasteboard boxes, on paper—even on Kleenex."

"The devil it does!" Drake said. "This is news to *me,* and I'm completely satisfied that Jordan doesn't know anything about it."

"He was trying to get her fingerprints," Mason said.

"Purely routine—probably in an attempt to break her down and get her to make some admission," Drake said. "That's one thing about Jordan, he's inclined to be a little heavy-handed. He takes jobs as a bodyguard, and they tell me he's inclined to be a little rough on occasion."

"All right," Mason said. "I just wanted the lowdown. I may have to sue the agency for a hundred thousand bucks for defamation of character."

"No skin off my nose," Drake told him. "Do you want I should do anything more about Sophia Atwood?"

"Not right now," Mason said. "Call your man in wherever he is, send him home, and send me a bill."

"Will do," Drake said, and hung up.

Mason went back to the automobile where Della Street was waiting.

Chapter 5

Stuart Baxley answered the doorbell.

He gazed incredulously at Mason and Della Street.

"*You*, back here!" he exclaimed.

Mason smiled. "In person. We wish to see Sophia Atwood."

"Sophia Atwood can see no one at the present time."

"Are you acting for her?" Mason asked.

"She is seeing no one."

"Then *she* hasn't told *you* that she wishes to see no one?"

"Of course she's told me."

"Then you're in touch with her?"

"All right, I'm in touch with her."

Mason said, "Della Street, my secretary, has an order from Katherine Ellis, an order permitting and directing Miss Street to pick up certain articles of wearing apparel from the room occupied by Katherine Ellis."

"Well, she can't come in the house," Baxley said.

"I would like to have that refusal come from Mrs. Atwood in person," Mason said. "I do not recognize any authority on your part."

"Try entering this house and you'll find my authority," Baxley blustered.

"I understand you are going to use force to prevent Miss Street from getting these clothes?"

"I'll use force," Baxley announced belligerently.

Jordan, the private detective, who had been attracted by the sound of the voices, came forward and said, "Mr. Baxley, may I talk with you for a moment?"

"In just a minute," Baxley said.

Mason said, "My client has been subjected to annoyance and humiliation. She has been falsely accused of crime. She has been ejected from the house where she is living, without her clothes. She wants her clothes. If I am not permitted to get those clothes, it will be an act in aggravation of damages. If I am permitted to get the clothes, it may be a circumstance which will be considered in mitigation of the resulting damages. I think Mrs. Atwood should know this."

"Just a minute, just a minute," Jordan said. "Wait there a minute." He took Baxley's arm, escorted him out of earshot. They talked in low voices for some two or three minutes. Then Baxley, apparently in an angry mood, withdrew, and Jordan came to the door.

"You and Miss Street may come in, Mr. Mason," he said. "If you'll wait in the library here, I'll show Miss Street where Katherine Ellis had her room. She can take whatever she desires, provided the authorization is in proper shape. We will, of course, assume no responsibility for what you folks are taking."

"Fair enough," Mason said. "Here is the authorization."

Jordan studied it for a few moments, then put it in his pocket.

"That authorization is to Mrs. Sophia Atwood," Mason pointed out.

"We're representing her," Jordan said. "Come in."

"I take it," Mason said, "your willingness to let Miss Street remove things means you've already searched Katherine Ellis' room?"

The detective grinned. "You are at liberty to draw your own conclusions."

They entered the house. Mason took a seat in the library. Jordan escorted Della Street up the creaking, old-fashioned staircase with its curved banister. Baxley was in some other part of the house.

A few moments later, there were light steps on the stairs and then Mason arose as an attractive woman entered the room.

"You're Mr. Mason?" she asked.

The lawyer bowed.

"I'm Sophia Atwood."

"I'm very glad to meet you," Mason said. "Inasmuch, however, as we are representing adverse interests and I am

37

an attorney, I would prefer that you have your legal representative here when I . . ."

"Oh, bosh!" she said. "Sit down, Mr. Mason. I want to talk with you."

"I am here as Katherine Ellis' attorney," Mason said.

"I know, I know, I know. You're getting ready to bring a suit for damages and all that. Just don't try to hold me responsible for anything Stuart Baxley has said."

"He isn't representing you?" Mason asked. "That is, he's not your agent in this matter?"

"He's *trying* to be my agent. He's giving me advice, telling me what to do and what not to do; but I'm going to do what I want to do, not what somebody else wants me to do."

"Do you really feel that Katherine Ellis has stolen money from you?" Mason asked.

"Now, that's what you lawyers would call a leading question," she said and smiled. "I'm not going to answer that right now. Anyway, what I believe doesn't make any difference."

"It is, of course, a matter of proof," Mason said. "And every citizen has constitutional rights, particularly in connection with an accusation of crime."

"Well," she said, "I don't mind telling you this. I have lived alone for a long time and I suppose that's made me a little suspicious of people and perhaps a little furtive.

"I had a hundred dollars in a hatbox in my closet on a shelf, I keep that closet locked. Someone got into that closet and took the hundred dollars out of the hatbox.

"I'm afraid I accused Stuart Baxley at first. And he was, of course, indignant and was the first to point out that, if it came to theft, Katherine was the one who had the most opportunity."

"In other words, *he* focused suspicion on Katherine and made an accusation?" Mason asked.

"Well, now, there again you're asking leading questions," she said. "I don't know as I care to discuss the matter, but I do want to get my hundred dollars back. To a woman in my position, a hundred dollars is a very large sum of money."

Her keen, gray eyes peered at the lawyer through steel-rimmed spectacles. "A *very* great sum of money," she repeated.

"It was exactly a hundred dollars?" Mason asked.

"Exactly a hundred dollars."

"You'd been saving it for some time?" Mason inquired.

"Now, I'm not going to discuss my personal finances, but I *will* tell you I'd been saving it for some time. I have a savings account at my bank. I put in five dollars every so often, and I've got about two hundred and fifty dollars in that account. I decided I wanted to go on a shopping splurge. I was going to get some clothes. I drew out a nice crisp one-hundred-dollar bill. I didn't want to carry that amount of money in my purse, so I placed it where I thought it would be safe in this hatbox in the closet."

"And when you came to look for it this evening the money was gone?"

"Exactly. And the hatbox had been knocked off on the floor. . . . Now, I understand this detective that Stuart Baxley got for me is going to be able to get fingerprints from that box. That is, he's trying to."

"How many people have handled the box?" Mason asked.

"I've handled it, if that's what you mean."

"And when you called Baxley's attention to the theft, he handled it?"

"He picked it up and looked it over to see if he could find any clues, yes."

"And the detective, Mr. Jordan, has handled it?"

"No, Mr. Jordan hasn't. He got a pair of pliers and picked it up with that."

"So you know that Stuart Baxley's fingerprints are on the box," Mason said.

"Yes."

"Then, if you find Katherine Ellis' fingerprints, you will discount the fact of Baxley's fingerprints also being on the box?"

"Well, of course, his had a right to be because he picked it up, whereas Katherine has absolutely no busisness in my closet."

"And if Katherine had been the one who was there and picked up the box and then you had found Stuart Baxley's fingerprints on it, that would make Baxley the thief?" Mason inquired.

She regarded him for a moment with penetrating gray eyes, then laughed and said, "You lawyers certainly do twist people up. I just wanted you to know that I'm trying to be fair, Mr. Mason. And so far *I* haven't accused Katherine of anything. I've just told you the facts."

"May I ask how it happens Stuart Baxley is representing you?" Mason inquired.

"He isn't."

"He said he was."

"He wants to, that's all. I'm representing myself."

"You've known him for some time, I take it?" Mason asked.

"Some time, yes."

"What does 'some time' mean?"

"It means some time."

"A year?"

"Not that long."

"A month?"

"Perhaps."

"And you are short only a hundred dollars?"

"Yes."

"You're certain it's exactly a hundred dollars?" Mason inquired again.

"That's right. A single crisp one-hundred-dollar bill."

"And the bank records will show where you made the withdrawal?"

"Certainly they will. When I tell you something, Mr. Mason, I tell you the truth. I don't believe in lying."

Again there were steps on the stairs. Della Street, followed by Levering Jordan, came down the stairs. Jordan was carrying a suitcase. Della Street was carrying an overnight bag.

Della Street said, "I've picked out some things that she'll be needing right away and I have her cosmetics, night things and enough to last her for a few days."

"Well, she can come and get the balance of her things at any time," Sophia Atwood said.

Mason said, "This is my secretary, Miss Street, Mrs. Atwood."

Sophia Atwood arose, walked over to Della Street, studied her closely. "I'm very pleased to meet you, Miss Street," she said, and held out her hand.

Della Street put down the bag in order to take Sophia Atwood's hand. "Thank you," she said. "The pleasure is mine. I had expected to find you—well, rather emotionally upset."

"I *am* upset," Mrs. Atwood said, "but I hope it's not going to affect my judgment or my manners. You're a very nice young woman, Miss Street. Nice appearing, nice spoken."

"Why, thank you!" Della Street said.

Mrs. Atwood turned to Mason.

"Mr. Mason," she said, "you're Katherine's attorney."

Mason nodded.

"I didn't know Katherine knew any lawyer here."

"She knows me."

"Prior to the time you came here?"

"Oh yes."

"How long have you known her?"

"Some time."

Mrs. Atwood laughed. "You're smart. Now, I'll ask you how long is 'some time'?"

"Some time."

Sophia said dryly. "And she telephoned you *immediately*—just as soon as she had a chance to get at a telephone."

"Many people telephone me, and at all hours," Mason said.

"I dare say they do. Well, Mr. Mason, I can understand your position. You don't want to talk with me if I am apt to be an adverse party in litigation where you are representing Katherine, but I do want to tell you that at no time did *I* ever accuse Katherine of any crime.

"I have simply stated facts. I had a hundred dollars which I withdrew from the savings account of my bank and put the

41

money in a hatbox on a shelf in a closet. When I unlocked the closet, the hatbox was on the floor and the money was gone.

"I also want to tell you that any accusations which were made by Stuart Baxley or Mr. Jordan were entirely the result of their own thinking and are entirely independent actions as far as I am concerned."

"Stuart Baxley is not your agent?" Mason asked. "He is not representing you?"

"Heavens, no!"

"Thank you," Mason said.

She smiled. "Well, I've said enough to you, Mr. Mason. I'm just going to tell you that, as far as I am concerned, I had nothing to do with the events which led to Katherine's departure. She can get her things any time she wishes to. I trust that you have enough things to last her for the next few days, Miss Street?"

"I think so."

"Because Katherine has a job, and I think it's important that she keep that job. My own idea is that work is the best medicine on earth. I wanted her to find some sort of work. I may have exerted subtle pressure to get her to find a job.

"And now I know you're anxious to rejoin your client and get her things to her. I can imagine how poor Kit feels. You tell her that her Aunt Sophia sends love and best wishes."

"And may I also tell her that you are convinced she had nothing to do with the theft of the money from the hatbox?"

"You may not!" Sophia Atwood snapped. "I am not prejudging any person either for guilt or for innocence. Facts are facts, as I always say; and you can't argue with facts. But you may be quite certain that *I* made no accusations. I wouldn't make any accusation until I had evidence to support it."

"Stuart Baxley is responsible for getting the private investigator on the job?" Mason asked.

"I'll give you my testimony when you get me on the witness stand, young man," Sophia Atwood said, her eyes twinkling. "In the meantime, I have told you what you may tell Kit.

"And now, you'll excuse me; because, after all, this has been a trying day and I am no longer a young woman."

She bowed, smiled, said, "This way please," and escorted Mason and Della Street to the door.

"Well?" Della asked as Mason was loading the suitcase into the automobile.

"Shrewd like a fox," Mason said. "You can figure out what happened. She had a fortune in currency stashed away in that closet. Either someone stole it or she had reason to believe that Kit had discovered the money and felt perhaps that there was danger Kit would report it to the Bureau of Internal Revenue.

"So what does she do? She cleans out all of the cash, goes to a bank where she has a savings account of two hundred and fifty dollars, draws out one hundred dollars so there is a record of the withdrawal, then dumps the open hatbox on the floor and starts screaming she has been robbed."

"Then you don't think somebody—perhaps Stuart Baxley—discovered the money and took it all?"

"In that event," Mason said, "Sophia Atwood would be acting far differently from the way she is now. A woman would hardly lose every cent she had in the world without yelling for the police and trying to locate the culprit and recover at least *some* of the money."

"Even if it meant trouble with the income tax people?"

"Even if it meant lots of trouble with the income tax people," Mason said. "She'd try to recover what she could and then argue about income tax."

"In other words then, Sophia is putting on an act?"

"The evidence would so indicate," Mason said, "provided, of course, Katherine Ellis is telling us the truth."

"Clients *have* been known to lie to us," Della Street pointed out.

"So they have," Mason agreed dryly.

They drove back to the motel, and Mason reported his conversation with Sophia Atwood to Katherine.

Katherine listened attentively, unpacking while she was listening.

Suddenly she turned to Della Street. "Did you see the plaid skirt on the hanger with the pink blouse?"

"Did you want that?" Della Street said. "Should I have brought it?"

"I was hoping you would. I almost telephoned you and then thought I hadn't better. I . . . I wanted to wear it tomorrow; but never mind. I have other clothes here. And I'd sure like to have my alligator-skin shoes. They're my working shoes. . . . Never mind, I'll get by in these blacks shoes I'm wearing."

"Remember," Mason said, "Sophia, herself, is very cordial. She says that you may come at any time to get the rest of your things. Only I think it's a good idea for you to have a witness present when you go. You'd better have someone accompany you.

"You can reach me any hour of the night through the Drake Detective Agency. They're open twenty-four hours a day.

"Now, you forget about all this and try to get some sleep."

"I'll try to sleep," she promised. "I'll never forget about it."

"Do the best you can," Mason said, patting her shoulder gently, "and keep in touch."

He turned to Della Street and nodded.

Chapter 6

It was shortly before noon the next day when Drake's code knock sounded on Mason's door.

Della Street opened the door and Drake said, "I have a couple of items to report, Perry. I thought you'd be interested in them and wanted to let you know."

"What are they?" Mason asked.

"Item one," Drake said, "Sophia Atwood was telling the truth. She withdrew one hundred dollars from the Sunset National Bank where she has a savings account. She had been depositing it at the rate of five dollars a month. Then she went there and withdrew a hundred dollars, asking for a nice crisp hundred-dollar bill."

Mason frowned.

"So," Drake said, "it would appear that Sophia was perhaps setting the stage for a theft, that she wanted it to be a theft of just a certain amount."

"That's one explanation," Mason said. "What's the other item, Paul?"

"Now, this may not have anything to it," Drake said. "It may be just prejudiced opinion, but I've been talking with the receptionist at the Gillco Manufacturing Company."

"Go ahead," Mason said.

"It's not always the same lady," Drake said.

Mason came erect in his chair. "What!"

"That's what the receptionist tells me," Drake said.

"Of course," Drake went on, "my informant can't be certain, but she seems to be a pretty observing individual. She says there are two women who sell pencils; that they both look alike and dress alike; that they wear very dark glasses, pretend to be blind—groping their way around with a cane; that they come to work in taxicabs. But this girl insists that their shoes are a giveaway; that one of them has

45

a bunion at the base of the right big toe and has to have a shoe that is specially built. The other one has perfect feet which are neatly shod.

"She has names for them. She calls one of them Mrs. Bunion-Foot and one of them Mrs. Neat-Foot."

"Has she ever told anyone about her observations?" Mason asked.

"The telephone operator there at the switchboard."

"Did you talk with this telephone operator yourself?"

"Gosh, no. There's a stockholders' meeting coming up and some stockholder is trying to stir up trouble. The phone lines are busy."

Mason said, "Paul, I want you to get an operative on the job down there at the Gillco Manufacturing Company and find out about this second person. We know one of them. Now, I want to find the identity of the second one.

"Don't, however, make the mistake of talking with the cabdrivers, because they may report it. I think we'll find that each of these women has a regular cabdriver who takes her to work and comes and picks her up. It may be the same driver for both women.

"What I want is to have a good operative with a car on the job and have him follow the taxicab when it takes the woman home. If there are two of them, we'll find out where the second one lives. . . . What are you grinning about?"

Drake said, "That's already been done."

"When?" Mason asked.

"As of an hour ago."

"Good work, Paul."

Drake said, "As soon as I found out about this double in the beggar business, I called the office and had an operative come down with a car. I told him to stay on the job until the blind beggar showed up and then follow her home.

"This young woman staying with Mrs. Atwood, a niece of hers named Katherine Ellis, is she our client?"

Mason thought a moment, then said, "Katherine Ellis—Kit, for short—is a waitress at one of the Madison Milestone restaurants, the Midtown Milestone.

"She's *my* client, but not *yours*. I'm picking up the tab on this job—at least for the present."

"Class?" Drake said.

"Plenty," Della Street said.

Drake observed, "This case may be a lot more complicated than it seems, Perry. I'd better meet your client."

Mason grinned. "You will, Paul—that is, if there are any future developments."

Drake left the office, and Mason said to Della Street, "Ring up Madison's Midtown Milestone. Ask for Kit Ellis. Tell them it's a business call and ask if she can come to the phone. If she can't, leave word for her to call Mason's office."

Della Street put through the call, made the request, said into the telephone, "I see. Thank you. Ask her to call Mr. Mason's office, if you will, please . . . You can't . . . I see . . . Thank you."

Della Street dropped the phone into its cradle, turned to Mason and said, "She's on duty. Waitresses can't take telephone calls when they're on duty and they can't have messages delivered."

Mason said, "Tell you what let's do, Della; let's go down there for lunch and we'll ask the headwaiter to have her assigned to our table. That will give us a chance to see what's doing.

"And you might ring up the Tracy outfit, Della. You know, the one who has the used-car lot. Tell him that I have a client who is going to be needing transportation; that she will probably buy a car within the next thirty days, but that I'd like to have him let her have a used car for five or six days so she can have transportation without going back and forth on the bus at all hours of the day. It isn't too safe for a woman out on the streets catching those midnight buses."

Della Street nodded, said, "The file number on this case is 'thirty-two, twenty-four, thirty-two.'"

"What's that?" Mason asked.

Della Street smiled. "I was just remarking that some people have it easier than others."

"Oh," Mason said, grinning. "I get you now. Well, you may have a point there, Della."

"Not a point, a curve," she said. "You want to ask Paul Drake to have lunch with us?"

47

Mason hesitated a moment, then grinned and said, "Let's not, Della. Let's see if Drake isn't eating at the Midtown Milestone. I think it would be nice just to happen to run into him there."

"Thirty-two, twenty-four, thirty-two," Della Street said, and busied herself with the telephone. "I'm getting Mr. Tracy for you."

Chapter 7

Mason said to the headwaiter, "We want lunch. Could we have one of Kit Ellis' tables?"

The headwaiter hesitated. "Only by waiting until one of her tables is empty, but they are full up now. . . . You're Perry Mason, aren't you?"

"That's right," Mason said.

"I know," the headwaiter said. "Friend of the boss. I'll see what I can do, Mr. Mason, but we assign tables to waitresses, not waitresses to tables. In that way we keep the work of a waitress concentrated in a given territory; otherwise they'd be moving all over the dining room and having to avoid each other.

"We cater to a businessman's luncheon. It's a big thing with us, and a good many of the people like to leave their offices, have lunch, and then get back to the office within an hour, so we try to keep things moving on an efficient basis."

"I know," Mason said. "How are the Ellis tables—all crowded?"

"They're all taken. A man came in here a few minutes ago and wanted one of her tables—the last one we had."

"We'll wait," Mason decided.

"All right. I'll put you in for the next vacancy in her tables, but it may be ten or fifteen minutes."

Mason said, "We'll go in the bar and sit down. Let us know when you have a table."

"Okay, I will," the headwaiter said.

Mason led the way into the bar.

"No cocktail," Della Street said firmly, shaking her head, "or I'll be falling asleep this afternoon with my head pillowed on my typewriter."

Mason nodded. "It's just a good place to sit and wait,

Della. We'll have a sour lemonade made with carbonated water."

"Cheat on mine," Della Street said, "and put some sugar in it."

"Sugar in both of them," Mason said.

They seated themselves in the bar. Mason gave the order, and they had their lemonades about half consumed when the loudspeaker said, "Mr. Mason's table is ready."

Della Street looked longingly at the lemonade—then using the straw, fished out the cherry and the slice of orange.

Mason paused to finish his drink, then escorted Della into the restaurant.

The headwaiter ushered them over to a table.

Kit Ellis came over to take their order. "Well, hello," she said.

She handed Della Street and Mason menus.

"The scallops are *particularly* good," Kit said. "I can recommend them."

"Scallops it is," Mason said.

Della Street nodded.

When Kit had moved away, Della Street moved closer to Mason, said, "Notice anything significant, Chief?"

"Such as what?" Mason asked.

"Shoes," Della Street said.

"What about the shoes?"

"She's wearing alligator-skin shoes," Della Street said. "You remember last night she was wearing black leather shoes and she asked me if I had thought to bring along the alligator-skin shoes. She said those shoes were her working shoes.

"I hadn't brought them. Then you remember she said it was all right, she'd work with her black shoes, but they weren't as comfortable. She must have stopped by the house and got her alligator shoes."

Mason frowned. "That would be a development," he said. "In that case she must have gone back and seen her aunt, and that might have considerable bearing on the case."

"Want to ask?" Della Street said.

Mason frowned. "Let's wait and let *her* tell *us*," he said.

Kit hurried past their table carrying a tray.

Mason's eyes were on the alligator shoes as Kit Ellis hurried by.

Della, reading his mind, said, "Madison evidently supplies them with smocks that are embroidered with the name of the restaurant. They put those smocks over their street clothes. Then he has a machine which embroiders a patch with their names. This is sewn to the smock."

Mason nodded.

"Of course, that's as far as the uniforms go," Della Street said. "They may wear their street clothes under the smock, or they may take off the outer garments, but the shoes and stockings are evidently the ones they come to work in."

"I presume," Mason said, "they have lockers. Those smocks may be too heavy to be worn over their regular clothes."

Della Street looked past Mason, said, "Oh-oh, here comes Paul. I'll bet he's looking for our file 'Thirty-two, twenty-four, thirty-two.' "

Mason grinned.

"No, he's looking for us," Della Street said. "He's got us spotted. Here he comes."

Paul Drake walked over to their table.

"Hi, Paul," Mason said. "Have a seat. Had lunch?"

"Not yet," Drake said. "I had an idea I might find you here."

"Something new?" Mason asked.

Drake said, "There's a report from my operative who is now at the Gillco Company. He says that the blind pencil seller is on the job. I had left instructions that he was to notice her feet particularly. He says this is Mrs. Bunion. She has a pronounced bunion at the base of the big toe on the right foot."

Della said, "Then it's another woman. I had occasion to look at Sophia Atwood yesterday. She had very neat feet and ankles."

"Paul, how do you keep in touch with your men on a job of this kind?" Mason asked.

"As I said before, some of the cars have field telephones

in them. The men can report directly to the office. But, for the most part, the cars we use for shadowing are just plain, ordinary, knock-around cars—just as average as we can get them. We get one of the popular makes that's about three or four years old, with no distinguishing marks, keep it a couple of years, and trade it in on another one. We use Tracy's Car Mart for replacements.''

"I've got my friend, Tracy, picking out a used car for my client in this case," Mason said. "I don't want her running around the city at night, taking buses.''

Drake sized Mason up, said, "You do all right for your clients. What will the income tax people say?''

Mason grinned. "We'll let Della Street handle that end of it, Paul. She has a string of figures that she uses in describing the account.''

Drake raised his eyebrows.

"Thirty-two, twenty-four, thirty-two," Della Street said.

Drake threw back his head and laughed.

Kit brought the scallops. Then Mason said, "I want some good ketchup, Kit, not this synthetic sauce that they ordinarily serve with scallops—and this is Paul Drake of the Drake Detective Agency. He's joining us for lunch.''

Drake acknowledged the introduction, regarded Katherine Ellis with quite evident approval.

"What's ready that's good?'' he asked.

"I'd recommend the scallops or the hot corned beef sandwich. They're both good. The sandwich will be quicker.''

"Bring me a hot corned beef sandwich, please," Drake said.

When Kit returned with the ketchup, Mason said, "I'm arranging for a car for you for at least a few days, Kit. I have a friend in the used-car business, and I'm getting you something you can use. It won't be anything fancy, but it'll be good transportation. And while you're staying there at the motel, I want you to use it. You're a little far from a bus line to suit me. Particularly on your late shifts.''

"Oh, Mr. Mason, how can I ever—I don't think I could afford to drive my own car. I . . .''

"This isn't your car," Mason said. "The tank's full of

gasoline. This car is a loan to you from me. You drive, I take it?"

"Oh, sure. I had my own car until . . . well, I had to sell it," she said, turning away quickly. She hurried to the kitchen counter with Drake's sandwich, and glided away.

Mason said, "Your men who don't have a phone in the car, Paul—how do *they* report to the office?"

"Well, a man can only sit in a car so long," Drake said. "Then he has to hunt up a rest room and, when he does, he telephones in. Of course, there's a chance he'll lose the subject while he's doing it; but it's the only way you can handle a deal of that sort, human nature being what it is. If you want a real shadow that is fool-proof, you need two men in two cars, and that's expensive.

"You'd be surprised, however, at how infrequently a person loses a subject. This is really good food!"

Mason nodded. "Madison does a good job. He tells me that he very seldom has to change his cooks. He keeps them happy and satisfied. Is this operative of yours the same man who shadowed Sophia Atwood yesterday?"

"Same one," Drake said.

"Any suspicion in his mind that it's not the same person?"

"I asked him particularly. He thinks it's the same person, but I told him to look carefully at the feet. He has a pair of binoculars with him. He says she has a bunion on the right foot."

"Then it's not Sophia Atwood," Della Street said positively.

"All right," Mason said to Paul Drake, "send another man down, Paul. We can't afford to lose this woman. Let's have two men on the job so we can be sure to find out who she is and where she goes."

Drake somewhat hurriedly finished his sandwich, said, "I'll leave you with the check, Perry. I'll hurry to the office and get another operative on the job."

"We'll tell Kit good-bye for you," Della Street said, smiling.

Drake took a half dollar from his pocket, put it under his

plate. "I'll tell her this way," he said, "and put it on the expense account."

Della Street and Mason finished their lunch, had a sherbet dessert, and returned to the office.

Drake's code knock sounded on the door within a matter of minutes after they had returned.

Della let the detective in, and Drake, his face grave, said, "There have been developments, Perry."

"What?"

"I just heard of them. Sophia Atwood is in the hospital in a critical condition."

"How come?"

"Somebody got in the house last night sometime, perhaps around midnight, knocked her out with a flashlight—one of those big five-cell outfits—and left her unconscious. The police discovered the crime about half an hour ago when Stuart Baxley went to the house.

"When no one answered his ring at the front door, he went around to the back door. He says he found the back door standing wide open. This aroused his suspicions and he went in and found Mrs. Atwood on the floor of the bedroom unconscious. The flashlight, which evidently had been used as a weapon, was lying beside her with the glass cracked. The surgeons say she has a subdural hematoma."

"She's still alive?" Mason asked.

"Apparently she's still alive, but in a deep coma."

"How did you hear about it?" Mason asked.

Drake said, "I have a confession to make, Perry. As soon as I reached the office, and knowing that the woman at the Gillco Manufacturing Company was not Mrs. Atwood, I sent an operative out to check on Sophia Atwood. I told him to go to the door, to pretend to be a door-to-door canvasser; to say that a neighbor had given him the name of Mrs. Atwood, and to try to sell her an encyclopedia or something of that sort. Our men all have a set of books and a line of descriptive patter that they can use on occasions of that sort. You'd be surprised, Perry. Sometimes we even get an order."

"And what happened?"

"My man got out there just after the ambulance had left.

Police were still prowling around, and he managed to get the story of what had happened. He got to a phone and called me."

"All right," Mason said. "This thing is deeper than I had imagined. I should have known when there was the discrepancy in the amount of cash on hand that . . ."

The lawyer abruptly stopped talking.

"Something I don't know?" Drake asked.

"Something you don't know," Mason told him, "and I don't want you to know. I'm getting a feeling about this case that makes me think we're headed for trouble and lots of trouble.

"Come on, Paul, let's get down to the Gillco Manufacturing Company and interview the woman who's selling pencils down there. You haven't had any reports that she's left?"

Drake shook his head.

Mason turned to Della Street. "You keep the store, Della. Give Tracy a ring. Tell him I want him to have that car ready for delivery at seven-thirty this evening. Say nothing about shoes to *anyone*, and I'll get back as soon as I can make it."

"Shoes?" Drake asked. "What about shoes?"

"Horseshoes," Mason told him, "for luck. Come on, Paul, let's go."

Chapter 8

The Gillco Manufacturing Company was out in a district where several factories had enough room to put in fenced parking lots for employees. The building was a three-storied structure designed for utility. Drake found a parking space at the curb, and he and Perry Mason entered the lobby where a good-looking woman in her thirties sat at the reception desk. Back of her was a switchboard where an operator was busily engaged in a hectic spurt of activity, plugging in lines, working keys.

Drake said, "Hello, I'm back again, and this time I've brought a friend with me."

She laughed. "Still interested in the blind woman who sells pencils? What are you—an officer trying to arrest her for begging or something?"

"No," Mason said, "we're just curious."

"Yes, I can understand," she said. "Just idle curiosity which brings two high-priced executives out here to . . . Say, aren't you Perry Mason, the lawyer?"

Mason nodded.

"Well, *that's* something!" she said. "Don't tell me this woman is mixed up in a murder case!"

"She may be a witness," Mason said. "Where is she?"

"Isn't she out there on the property line?"

Drake shook his head. "She's not in her accustomed place."

"She must have left then. I know she was there about half an hour ago."

"The property line?" Mason asked.

"It's just off the sidewalk and she's on the property of the manufacturing company. It's really outside the jurisdiction of the city and is private property. Mr. Gillman said to leave her there—for luck."

"How can she make a living selling pencils there?" Mason asked.

"They're good pencils, that's why. She also has some ballpoint pens—some *really* good stuff, and—well, quite a few of the employees stop to buy from her. You'd really be surprised. Sometimes I think she does a pretty good business, but certainly not enough to warrant her using taxicabs."

"How else would she get out here?" Mason asked. "She could hardly come on a bus. If she's blind, she couldn't walk; and it's cheaper to get a taxi than to try and hire a car and driver."

"I know," the woman said. "I asked her once why she came by cab and got just about the same answer. She also said that the cab companies make a special rate to blind people who have to go out to different stations like that—or the drivers do, or something. Anyway, she said she got a special rate."

"How long has she been coming?"

"A little over two weeks."

"You noticed her feet, Mr. Drake tells me," Mason said.

"That's right. There are actually two women. One of them has very neat feet. The other one has a pretty good left foot, but the right foot has a bunion."

"How did you happen to notice that?"

"Oh, I just notice things. Tell me—I'm giving you lots of information; I don't know whether Mr. Gillman would like it or not—would you like to talk with him and ask him if it's all right? I don't like to . . . Well, I know Mr. Gillman wouldn't want me to say anything that would attract any undue amount of attention to the company."

"Sure thing," Mason said. "May we go up to his office?"

"Just a moment," she said, and picked up a phone.

She waited a full thirty seconds before getting a line, then said, "Mr. Gillman's office, please . . . Hello, could Mr. Gillman see Mr. Perry Mason, the lawyer?"

A moment later she smiled at Mason. "I'm sorry. Mr. Gillman's tied up, with people waiting to see him and a whole string of phone calls he has to make within the next two hours.

"It's a very busy time of year for him."

She dropped the phone into place.

She looked questioningly at Paul Drake. "Are you also a lawyer, Mr. Drake?"

"A private detective," Mason said, "who is checking on a matter for me."

"Involving the blind beggar?"

"We don't know," Mason told her. "We've had some leads in that direction. That's all we know and we'd like to find out more about her. But please don't let her know we're investigating.

"My," she said, "it's mysterious!"

Abruptly she looked behind them to a young man who had come hurrying in carrying a briefcase.

"Mr. Gil—" he began, but the receptionist interrupted him.

"Go right up, Mr. Deering. He's waiting for you."

She turned back to Mason as the young man hurried to the elevators.

"Is it something important?"

Mason smiled and bowed. "It's just a routine matter. Thank you very much. You've been most helpful."

"You're leaving me out on the end of a limb," she protested.

Mason laughed good-naturedly. "Don't worry. We'll subpoena you as a witness."

She made an exaggerated grimace of distaste. "You do and I'll shoot you," she said.

Mason and Drake walked out of the reception room and exchanged brief significant glances.

"Now what?" Drake asked.

"Evidently she's left and your two operatives are tailing her. Let's get to a telephone booth, Paul, and see if they've made a report."

"Well, things certainly do take on a peculiar aspect here," Drake said. "Look here, Perry, you know something I don't know about this case. You know something about a sum of money."

58

"Possibly," Mason said.

"Going to tell me?"

"No."

"Why?"

"It's best that you know only what I tell you about this case," Mason said, weighing his words carefully. "I'll tell you this much—the receptionist addressed that young man who came in as Deering. If it should happen his first name is Hubert, that might be very significant.

"So you and I are going to jot down the numbers on the license plates of the automobiles parked out front; then later on you're going to check the ownership of those cars.

"As soon as we've got those license numbers, let's get to a phone, call your office and see what's new."

There were a dozen cars parked at the curb. Mason took one end of the line, Drake the other. They quickly wrote down the license numbers of the parked cars, then drove to a service station which had a phone booth, and Drake called his office.

When Drake came back to the car, he was thoughtful. "We've run Mrs. Bunion down to earth," he said. "A flat, an old district down Santa Monica way. She's a blind recluse who has lived there for more than two years. *Her* name, incidentally, is Gillman."

"Gillman?" Mason said. "Any relation to Gillman at the Gillco Company?"

"I'm giving you what information I have," Drake said. "Her name is Gillman. She's been living in this flat. She's eccentric. Sometimes people don't see her for two or three days. Then she'll come along the sidewalk waving her cane in front of her, going to the corner market.

"They know her well at the corner market. She pays cash. Quite frequently they carry the provisions for her. A blind woman, living all alone, doing her own cooking—that represents a problem."

"Well," Mason said, "we'll start asking questions. What would you do, Paul, if you were blind and had a limited income? You wouldn't dine out. You couldn't hire a cook."

"You have a point there," Drake said. "So what do we do?"

Mason said, "We keep your men on the job. When the blind woman comes out I want to know where she goes. I want to find out everything I can about her."

Drake said, "My operative thinks she knew she was being tailed right at the last."

"What makes him think so?" Mason asked. "After all, shadowing a blind woman shouldn't . . ."

Drake said, "It wasn't the woman who spotted the tail, it was the taxi driver. Some of those drivers get mighty skillful, and this driver was evidently good. My men had him bracketed, that is, one of them had moved on ahead of the cab and was watching in the rearview mirror, and the other one was tailing the cab. They'd swapped positions once or twice on the trip. That's good shadowing technique. One car passes, the other car drops behind. In that way the driver of the subject car doesn't realize there's a car on his tail."

"But this taxi driver did?" Mason asked.

"This taxi driver did. That is, my operative thinks so because he turned and said something to his passenger. After that the woman passenger sat stiffly erect.

"My operative thinks that the driver spotted the tail and told her that she was being followed."

"Let your operative stay on the job," Mason said. "We'll go to my office from here, but I want the names of the owners of those cars parked in front of the Gillco plant."

Drake relayed instructions to his operative, and they drove back to Mason's office quietly thoughtful.

At the office Mason said, "Ring up Kelsey Madison at Madison's Midtown Milestone, Della. I want to talk with him about his waitress."

Della Street nodded and a few moments later said, "Mr. Madison on the line, Chief."

Mason picked up his telephone, said, "Hello, Kelsey. How's business down there?"

"Same as usual," Madison said. "We're over the rush of the lunch hour. We'll have a cocktail rush at the bar and some early diners."

"You've got a waitress there—Katherine Ellis," Mason

said. "I'd like to talk with her. Would it be all right if she took about an hour off? This should be during the slack time."

"For you, Counselor, it would be a pleasure," Madison said. "Where do you want her?"

"Up at my office."

"She'll be there."

"It won't inconvenience you?"

"Not at all. We can double up on any business that's coming in now . . . Say, wasn't she the same waitress who waited on you a couple of days ago?"

"That's right."

Madison's voice suddenly became hard. "She didn't proposition you, did she, Perry?"

"No," Mason said, "I propositioned her."

Madison laughed. "That's all right, then. That's a customer's prerogative. I'll tell her to get on up there."

"Thanks," Mason said.

The lawyer hung up the phone, got up from his desk, walked over to the window and stood staring moodily down at the street. At length he turned and said, "You're sure about the shoes, Della?"

"I'm sure about the shoes."

Mason said, "Anything you hear as my secretary is a confidential privileged communication. Anything you see with your own two eyes is something different; you become a witness. What you have seen is evidence. It's illegal to suppress evidence—but we have to be mighty sure it *is* evidence."

The lawyer turned back from the window, started pacing the office floor, his head thrust slightly forward, his eyes on the carpet.

Della Street—knowing the symptoms of intense concentration on the part of her employer—sat perfectly still, doing nothing to distract his attention.

Chapter 9

It was three-thirty when Della, answering the telephone from the reception desk, said to Mason, "Katherine Ellis is here."

"Tell her to come in," Mason said.

Katherine Ellis entered the inner office with a smile for Della Street and then crossed over to stand opposite Perry Mason.

"What is it, Mr. Mason?" she said. "Mr. Madison said I was to come up here."

Mason nodded. "Sit down, Katherine. We've just got back from a little trip of exploration—Paul Drake and I."

"You mean something connected with the case?"

"Yes."

"Did you learn anything?"

"Let me ask you a few questions first?" Mason said. "Have you heard anything from your aunt today?"

She shook her head.

"Have you heard anything about her?"

"About her? Why? Is there something I should know?"

"Your aunt," Mason said, "was assaulted sometime last night—apparently by an intruder who struck her over the head with a big five-cell flashlight and . . ."

"That big flashlight!" she exclaimed. "Why, that's *my* flashlight!"

Mason regarded her thoughtfully.

"How is she, Mr. Mason? Is she badly hurt? Good heavens, I must go to her. Is she at home or . . ."

"She was in the receiving hospital the last I heard," Mason said, "in a coma. Apparently she'd been unconscious for some hours.

"Doctors say there's a blood clot on the brain of a type known as a subdural hematoma. This is a clot which is quite

62

frequently fatal and can be brought on, particularly in an aged person, by a blow on the head. The clot forms under the lining of the skull and brings pressure to bear on the brain. Moreover, if the clot is venous blood, the injury may reopen from time to time, causing more blood to infiltrate into the clot.''

She was watching Mason with wide startled eyes.

"Now then," Mason said, "when was the last time you saw your aunt?"

"Why, you know—when I left the house."

Mason shook his head.

"What do you mean shaking your head?" she asked.

Mason said. "We left you at the motel. Sometime after we left you went back to your aunt's house."

"How do you know?" she asked. "Did you . . . did the taxi . . . ?"

"I know," Mason said, "and probably the police will know, because of your shoes and the clothes you're wearing—the plaid skirt.

"You asked Della Street particularly about the alligator-skin shoes. Those were your working shoes. Being on your feet as much as you are there at the restaurant and not being accustomed to handling the job as waitress, you were having lots of trouble with your feet.

"When Della Street went to get your things, you forgot to tell her about your shoes; and when Della brought your things to you, you asked particularly about the alligator-skin shoes. Della told you she hadn't brought them. Yet this noon when you were waiting on the tables, you were wearing them.

"That very definitely means that you went to the house and got those shoes before you went to work. Now, did you do it early this morning or late last night?"

"I did it late last night," she said. "Oh, Mr. Mason, this is terrible!"

"All right," Mason said, "you did it late last night. How late?"

"It was after you had left the motel—probably a couple of hours. I tried to sleep. I kept thinking about how my feet were going to be killing me if I tried to wait tables in those black shoes. And then I realized I had a key to the house and I could run up and get my shoes and get out, all in a matter of minutes. Particularly if Aunt Sophia was asleep."

Mason said, "You'd better give me that key, Katherine."

She opened her purse, handed the lawyer a key.

"Now," Mason went on, "tell me, just what did you do?"

"I took some of the money that you had left with me for taxi fare. I called a taxi and had him wait down in front of the house. I used my key and went in. The house was dark and silent. I slipped off my shoes and went upstairs in my stocking feet. I didn't hear a sound."

"What did you do for light?"

"I just groped my way up the stairs and along the upper corridor until I got to my room. Then I switched on the light, picked up my alligator shoes, this plaid skirt and some clothes that I thought I would be wanting, turned out the light and groped my way to the turn in the upper corridor, then went down the stairs and out the front door. I wasn't in the house more than three or four minutes altogether."

"You say that big flashlight is yours?"

"Yes, I had a big five-cell flashlight which someone before me had had in the room where I was sleeping. I took the old batteries out of it, put fresh batteries in, and used that flashlight at night after Aunt Sophia had gone to bed. In that way I didn't need to turn on the corridor lights when I got up and awaken Aunt Sophia. Can you find out how she is, Mr. Mason?"

The door from the outer office opened and Police Lt. Tragg came walking in. "How do you do, Della," he said. "Hello, Perry. You'll pardon me coming in unannounced this way, but there's always a tendency on the part of attorneys to leave me cooling my heels in the outer room if I announce myself. The taxpayers don't like to have me waste my time, and I don't like to talk with a suspect who has been coached.

"I take it from the description I have that this is Katherine Ellis. And I'm sorry to state that I have a warrant for your arrest, Miss Ellis. I wish to advise you at this time that any statement you may make will be held against you: that you are not required to make any statement; that you are entitled to the services of an attorney at all stages of the proceeding."

"And the nature of the charge?" Mason asked.

Lt. Tragg's face was grave. "The nature of the charge," he said, "is assault with intent to commit murder, and the charge may be changed to murder.

"Sophia Atwood has taken a turn for the worse. She's not expected to live," Lt. Tragg went on.

Mason turned to Katherine Ellis. "You will," he cautioned, "say absolutely nothing. You will not answer any questions except when I am present and give you permission to speak. This is a serious matter and there are some things on which I don't want you to comment."

"If it's the nocturnal trip she made to the house with the taxi last night, Perry, we know all about it," Lt. Tragg said cheerfully. "One of the neighbors happened to hear the taxi drive up and stay there with the motor running. So, knowing there had been some commotion over there earlier in the evening, the neighbor got the number of the cab.

"We were able to find the cabby and he remembered the occasion of picking up Miss Katherine Ellis at the motel, taking her to the house, and waiting there while she ran inside and picked up some things. The records show she was in there about seven minutes.

"That was shortly after midnight, and the probabilities are that Sophia Atwood received her injuries at just about the time Miss Katherine Ellis was there with the taxicab waiting outside.

"That much I can tell you, Perry, because you'll be reading it in the paper.

"There are other things which I don't feel I should tell you at the present time, but they will have a bearing on the case.

"Now, I'm sorry, Miss Ellis, but you're going to have to come with me. We'll try to make the procedure as painless as possible. I'll have to have my hand on your arm, but we're not going to use handcuffs or anything like that; and we'll try and have as little publicity as possible—although, of course, newspaper reporters will be waitig for you at the station when we come in.

"If you want a suggestion from a much older man, I would suggest you do nothing to try to avoid the cameras but hold your chin up and your shoulders back, and very definitely don't try to hide your face. Give the photographers just as good a likeness as possible. I think Perry Mason will agree with me. It's better public relations.

"And now, if you're ready . . ."

Mason said, "Remember what I told you, Katherine. Say nothing, absolutely nothing! Make no statements of any sort. This is a serious charge and you'll have some enemies who will do all they can to get you convicted."

Mason crossed to her side. She clung to his arm in a panic. "But, Mr. Mason, I . . . I can't . . ."

Mason gently disengaged her clutching fingers. "Yes, Katherine," he said, "you have to. But I'll be in touch with you, and it isn't going to be quite as bad as you may think if you just keep your courage."

Chapter 10

Within minutes after Lt. Tragg had escorted Katherine Ellis from the office, Mason's unlisted phone rang and Drake said, "A check of those license numbers we took shows that one of the cars is registered in the name of Hubert Deering, Perry.

"The address is an apartment house at 965 Hempsted. Want to talk with him?"

"Not right now," Mason said. "Let's go see Mrs. Bunion. I'll pick you up at your office and we'll go see what she knows.

"My client has been arrested for assault with intent to commit murder, and that changes the picture a lot. Speed becomes essential.

"You have about three minutes before I get down there to call for you.

"Use that time to start an operative finding out what he can about a Bernice Atwood living at Palm Springs. She's the first wife of Gerald Atwood, deceased."

"And Sophia is the second wife?" Drake asked.

"Presumably," Mason said.

"Get some men working on it, Paul, and I'll be by for you in a matter of minutes."

Mason hung up the phone and a couple of minutes later picked up Paul Drake at the offices of the Drake Detective Agency.

The two men drove to the three-story flat in the rather dingy district. The operative Drake had kept on the job watching the place stepped on his brake briefly as the men drove up, the brake light signaling the operative had spotted them.

Drake said, "Do you want to risk going over and talking with my operative, Perry?"

Mason shook his head. "Let's go talk with the woman herself, and then we'll check with your operative later on."

"Okay," Drake said, and paused while he lit a cigarette.

"That's the signal to the operative," he said, "to stay on the job and sit tight."

The two men approached the apartment house. Mason picked the bell button for the middle apartment and pressed it.

Far upstairs they could hear a faint whir, but the speaking tube by the side of the door remained silent.

Mason waited a moment, then rang the buzzer again. When there was still no answer, the lawyer said, "Paul, we may be too late at that. Let's walk over and see your man."

They crossed the street to where Drake's operative was sitting in the car.

"She didn't go out?" Mason asked.

The man shook his head. "Not since I've been here."

"Anybody go in?"

"No one."

Mason and Drake exchanged glances.

"Of course," Drake pointed out, "she may not care for visitors. After all, Perry, she lives up one flight of stairs, and the probabilities are she's persisted to death with salesmen—people selling books, people selling insurance, people soliciting funds for this, that and the other charity and . . ."

"I know," Mason interrupted, "but she's part of the team. She is working with Sophia Atwood, and Sophia Atwood has been attacked. The woman may be in danger."

"Think we should notify the police?" Drake asked nervously.

"Only as a last resort," Mason replied. "We may have to, but I want to get into that flat and take a look around. I want to talk with her if she's alive—and if she isn't, I want to get a quick look at things before the police get on the job."

"That's dangerous," Drake pointed out.

"Lots of things I do are dangerous," Mason retorted as he started back across the street.

Again the lawyer pressed the button and listened for the buzzer.

"There's this speaking tube," Mason said. "She can call down to find out who's here and press a button which releases the catch on the door so anyone she wants to see can come up. Or if she wants to make it a short visit, she can come down and slide that little panel in the door and talk through this six-inch square opening."

"Or," Drake commented dryly, "she can do none of those things and simply sit tight. What would you do if you were blind and living by yourself in a city?"

Mason thought that over, then said, "I probably wouldn't answer the door either."

The lawyer placed his mouth at the opening of the speaking tube. "Oh, Mrs. Gillman!" he called. "Mrs. Gillman, we want to see you on a matter of some importance."

There was no answer.

The lawyer gave a shrill whistle, raised his voice. "Oh, Mrs. Gillman! We have a matter of importance to discuss with you, Mrs. Gillman."

Abruptly the door of the lower flat opened two or three inches to the end of a safety chain which stretched taut across the opening. A woman's authoritative voice, high-pitched with emotion, said, "What's the meaning of all this commotion? I'm the manager here. What's going on?"

Mason said, "I'm sorry. We want to see Mrs. Gillman on a matter of some importance. I believe she's home, but she isn't answering her doorbell."

"Of course she isn't answering her doorbell," the woman said. "Why should she? She doesn't have any friends to call on her. And why should she go traipsing up and down stairs for people who want to talk to her about things in which she isn't interested? As a matter of fact, she's blind and living by herself. Now, you folks just go away and quit making this unearthly racket."

Mason said, "I'm sorry. My name is Mason. I'm an attorney."

"*Perry* Mason?" the woman asked.

"That's right."

"Well, what do you know!" the woman exclaimed, and then after a moment added, "I declare!"

"And this," Mason said, "is Paul Drake who is associated with me in some investigative work."

"What do you mean 'investigative work'?" the woman asked shrewdly. "Is he a private detective?"

"That's right, ma'am," Drake said.

"Well, what in the world do you people want with Mrs. Gillman?"

"We want to talk to her," Mason said. "It's vitally important."

"Important to whom, to you or her?"

"It may be *very* important to her," Mason said.

"Well, there's certainly something mysterious going on. You people have been walking back and forth across the street and talking with the man over there in that car. Who is that man?"

"He is one of Mr. Drake's assistants," Mason said. "We have a feeling that Mrs. Gillman may be in some danger, and we would like to warn her."

"Warn her!" The manager's voice became shrill. "What good does it do to warn a blind woman that she's in danger? What good would *that* do?"

Mason was silent.

"Put yourself in her shoes," the woman went on. "She's completely blind, living in total darkness in a big city, and you two come along and tell her she's in danger. What good does a warning like that do? If she's in danger, go to the police."

"We *may* be in a position to help her," Mason said. "We might be in a position to post a guard."

"And who's going to pay for all that?"

"We would."

"I see," the woman said thoughtfully.

"Now, then," Mason went on, with his most disarming smile, "how is the best way for us to reach her?"

"I'll reach her for you," the woman said.

"That's fine. I take it you have a passkey?"

"I don't need a passkey. I'll call her on the telephone."

"She has a phone?" Mason asked.

"Of course she has a telephone. A blind woman, living by herself, couldn't get along without a telephone. But it's an unlisted number and I'm about the only one who has that unlisted number. Now, you just wait right there and I'll go and call her and ask her if she'll see Mr. Perry Mason and—what's that other name?"

"Paul Drake."

"All right, I'll go and see if she'll talk with you."

The woman paused a moment, then added, "My name is Minerva Gooding. I'm the manager of these flats. I live in the lower flat and rent out the two upper flats. They aren't very swank, but it's a nice, comfortable house. Now, you wait right there where you are and I'll go talk with her."

Mrs. Gooding was gone some three minutes, then returned to the door.

"I'm sorry," she said, "but Mrs. Gillman doesn't answer the telephone."

"She doesn't answer!" Mason repeated.

Mrs. Gooding shook her head.

"Well, she isn't answering the doorbell either," Mason said.

"That's customary, but she *always* answers the telephone when she's in because she knows that I'm about the only one who has the unlisted number. She has one other woman who I think calls her, but I don't know who she is."

"Would it be a Mrs. Atwood?" Mason asked.

"Atwood . . . Atwood . . . Now, that name sounds kind of familiar. I've heard her talk about an Atwood. Would her first name be Sophia?"

Mason nodded.

"Well, I've heard her talk a lot about a Sophia—but whether it's Sophia *Atwood* or not, I don't know. But anyway, she isn't answering the telephone."

"Then something is wrong," Mason said, "because she's home."

"How do you know she's home?"

"We're pretty certain. That man sitting in the automobile across the street has been keeping an eye on the place," Mason said, and then added hastily, "to see that she wasn't in any danger until we could warn her."

"What sort of danger?" Mrs. Gooding snapped.

"Frankly," Mason said, "we don't know, but we do have reason to believe that she may have something someone wants—someone who is unscrupulous and who would be willing to break into a house in order to get it."

Mrs. Gooding thought that over.

"Well," she said at length, "I'll take the passkey and run up there and see if she's all right. You'll wait right here."

"We'd like to go with you," Mason said. "If anything has happened, it would be a very good idea for you to have witnesses."

"Witnesses to what?"

"Witnesses to what you found."

"All right," Mrs. Gooding said after a moment's hesitation, "come along, but don't touch anything, and I don't want you folks making any criticism.

"Land sakes, you just figure that *you're* blind and living all alone. You have your own cooking to do and have your own dishes to wash, your own clothes to put away, your own bed to make, and you have to get around by yourself. It's a job just to keep yourself lined up with things so you know where you are and don't get mixed up on directions.

"You can't keep a neat, orderly house working like that. You just have to live from hand to mouth and take things the way they come. Now, I want you to understand that and not make any criticisms."

"We understand," Mason said. "We're not interested in her housekeeping or her neatness."

"And," Mrs. Gooding went on, "when you talk with her, I don't want her alarmed, you understand? You can tell me about her being in danger, but I don't want her frightened to death. Think what it's like to be living in perpetual night all the time. You can't tell if a person is crawling toward your bed with a knife in his hand when you wake up at night. There are lots of things you can get yourself adjusted to, but you can't get yourself adjusted to terror.

"Now, you come with me and stay right behind me. I don't you want you wandering around at all, and I want you to remember the circumstances under which Edith Gillman has to live.

"Once in a while I come in and help her clean up and shovel out some of the stuff, but you can't—well, for instance, take sweeping. When you're blind, you can't sweep a room, pick up the dirt in a dustpan, put it anywhere, and do a neat job. You just have to live with things the way they are.

"Now, you both come along with me, and stay behind me."

She opened the front door of the lower flat, took a passkey from her purse, fitted it to the door leading to the second-story flat, and Mason and Paul Drake followed her up the stairs.

The place had a stale, musty smell which assailed their nostrils as they climbed the stairs. They paused at a central reception hallway at the top of the stairs. Mrs. Gooding said, "Heaven knows whether these lights are on or not."

"She keeps the electricity on because she uses it to cook with, but electric lights don't mean anything to her, so they're just as apt as not to be all burned out."

She clicked a switch as she talked. Lights turned on to show a bedroom arranged with Spartan simplicity. There was a dresser and there were no ornaments on the dresser. The chairs were pushed back against the wall so the center of the room was free of obstructions. The bed was at the far side of the room by the window. The bed had not been made. The sheets were rumpled; the pillows were in a compact group at the corner of the bed.

"You see what I mean," Mrs. Gooding said. "She didn't have time to make her bed."

She raised her voice. "Oh, Edith, *yoo-hoo!* This is Minerva. Where are you?"

She paused and waited for an answer. Then, when there was no answer, she frowned and repeated the call in a louder voice.

"Edith, *yoo-hoo! Yoo-hoo!*"

Mrs. Gooding said, "You folks stay *right* here. I'm going to look around."

"Can't we help you?" Mason asked.

"You can not. This place is in no condition for visitors, and Edith is going to be good and mad at me for bringing you up here. You get out of this bedroom. Come in here and sit down and stay put."

She led the way into a sitting room in which there was one comfortable chair with a radio on a table by the chair.

"Poor dear has nothing to do except sit here and listen to the radio," Mrs. Gooding said. "She knows all the voices, all the actors. And the way that woman keeps up with the news—you'd really be surprised.

"Now, don't touch anything," Mrs. Gooding warned again.

Drake and Mason stood in the center of the room. They heard Mrs. Gooding moving through the flat, calling from time to time, "Edith, yoo-hoo, this is Minerva. Where are you, Edith? Are you all right?"

After some two or three minutes Mrs. Gooding came back to the living room. "Well," she said, "she isn't here. She must have gone out."

"I'm sorry," Mason said, "she couldn't have gone out. We've had this man on duty out front."

"Does he know her when he sees her?" Mrs. Gooding asked.

"Yes."

"How does that happen?"

"He has seen her several times before," Mason explained noncommittally. "Tell me, is there a back door?"

"Of course there's a back door. I wouldn't let any person live in a flat which only had one exit. What would a body do in case of fire?"

"Where's the back exit?" Mason asked.

"It goes down a flight of stairs to the alley. There's a little service porch in back."

"Did you look on the service porch?" Mason asked.

"No," she said, "I didn't, but I will. You wait right there."

She hurried through the flat; after a few moments she came back and said, "Well, I'll say this—the back door was unlocked. Apparently she went out the back door down the steps to the alley."

"And then what?" Mason asked.

"Well," Mrs. Goodling said, and hesitated.

"Yes?" Mason prompted.

"Sometimes," Mrs. Goodling said, "she telephones her friend—this one she calls Sophia—and Sophia will come and get her in the alley."

"Why in the alley?" Mason asked.

"You can search me," Mrs. Gooding said. "I'm not inclined to inquire into other people's business. I just happened one time to go out on my back porch to put some stuff in the garbage pail and I saw Edith Gillman coming down the back stairs, feeling her way along, and this Cadillac automobile was there in the alley with the motor running and a chauffeur. I think it was a hired car, if you know what I mean; and this woman was halfway up the steps ready to assist Edith down. And I heard Edith say, 'How are you today, Sophia?' And, believe me, that was *all* I heard.

"I made certain I didn't hear any more. If she wanted to be secretive about some of her friends, it was all right with me."

"I see," Mason said. And then after a moment he added, "You're absolutely certain she's not in the flat now?"

"I've looked everywhere except under the bed."

"Then," Mason said gravely, "let's look under the bed."

"Why in the world would she be under the bed?"

"I don't know," Mason said. "But why should she come home, enter the flat by the front door, go down the rear stairs to the alley and be whisked off in a rented car?"

'Well, if she did, it's her business, not ours."

"Nevertheless," Mason said, "it's up to us to make certain she isn't here."

"She wouldn't have crawled under any bed."

"Someone might have hit her over the head and pushed the body under the bed," Mason said.

"Bosh and nonsense!"

"For your information," Mason said, "her friend, Sophia Atwood, was also living alone, and last night someone entered the house, hit Mrs. Atwood over the head, and went away and left her lying there on the floor."

Mrs. Gooding stood looking at them with startled, incredulous eyes. "You mean Edith Gillman's friend?"

"I don't know," Mason said. "I'm trying to find out. But we had reason to believe that Mrs. Gillman was friendly with Sophia Atwood."

"Well, I'll declare," Mrs. Gooding said in a subdued tone.

"You found the back door unlocked?" Mason asked.

"Yes, there's a key lock on the door. It's not a spring lock. You have to turn a key to lock the door. Now, she must have been in a hurry when she left because she didn't take the back-door key with her. The back-door key is on the inside of the door, and the door's unlocked."

"That's not usually the case?" Mason asked.

She looked at him and said, "If you were blind, would you be living in a place with the doors unlocked?"

"No," Mason said shortly.

Paul Drake said, "Of course, someone could have been waiting and hustled her out through the back door in a hurry, telling her it was important—someone she knew."

"Or," Mason added dryly, "someone she *didn't* know. Who has the third-story flat, Mrs. Gooding?"

"It's vacant at the moment."

"Would you mind if we looked at it?" Mason asked.

"Not at all. But you'll have to go all the way back down the stairs to the front door, then climb two more flights of stairs."

"I'd like to take a look," Mason said. "It's unfurnished?"

"That's right."

"I'd like to get an idea of the way it's laid out. It has the same floor plan as this one?"

"Yes."

"May we look?"

Mrs. Gooding said, "Just follow me, please," and led the way down the stairs. She held the front door of the flat open for them, then closed it as they left, inserted the passkey into the door leading to the third-floor flat, opened it and said, "Here's where we start climbing stairs. You don't mind?"

"Not at all," Mason said.

The trio climbed the two flights of stairs, and again Mrs.

Gooding brought a passkey into play as she opened a locked door at the head of the stars.

Mason and Drake moved through the empty flat, then nodded to Mrs. Gooding. "Thank you very much, Mrs. Gooding," Mason said. "We'll be leaving. If Mrs. Gillman should return, would you mind calling Paul Drake at the Drake Detective Agency?"

"I'll do nothing of the sort," Mrs. Gooding snapped. "I'm not going to spy on any of my tenants for . . ."

"I didn't mean it that way," Mason said. "The woman is blind. Quite obviously it wouldn't do any good to leave a card for her and ask her to call the Drake Detective Agency."

"Oh, I see," Mrs. Gooding said. "I'll tell you what I'll do. I'll give her the number when she comes. I'll tell her that you gentlemen were looking for her—but I'm not going to alarm the poor soul—and I'll ask her to call you. I'll give her the number."

"Could she remember the number," Mason asked, "if you gave it to her . . . ?"

"Could she remember it!" Mrs. Gooding exclaimed. "You should see the memory that woman has. She can remember telephone numbers for weeks. She has the most phenomenal ability to recall—and the way she's posted on current events, on news and things, is absolutely startling."

"Very well," Mason said, "we'll leave it at that."

"Understand now, I'm not going to alarm her."

"We don't want you to. And thank you very much indeed for your co-operation."

"I think perhaps," Mrs. Gooding said, "I should be thanking you—on behalf of Edith Gillman—but I'll wait until I know more than I do now."

Mason and Paul Drake left the flat building, moved across the street to their automobile.

"Well?" Drake asked.

"Either something has happened to her," Mason said, "or she's playing a pretty deep game."

"What's our next move, Perry?"

"I want *two* operatives," Mason said, "one watching the front, and one watching the rear, and notify me just as soon as she returns to the flat. While we were looking around upstairs I managed to get the unlisted number of the telephone by copying the number shown in the circular window and . . ."

Drake laughed. "We'd better get our signals together, Perry. I, too, was busy copying that number."

"All right," Mason said, "we both have it. Now, then, if she comes home we'll call her on her unlisted telephone and see if we can arrange an interview. In any event, we'll be able to warn her."

"And in the meantime?" Drake asked.

"In the meantime," Mason said, "we are one jump ahead of the police as far as the two blind beggars are concerned. We'll try and stay one jump ahead of the police.

"If the blind woman with the bunion, Mrs. Gillman, is in any danger, someone is going to come to her house looking for her."

"Unless someone was waiting in the house when she got home and spirited her out of the back door," Drake said.

"That," Mason said, "is always the possibility. But if so, why did they do it?"

Drake shrugged. "You've got me."

Mason said, "If they had just wanted to kill her, they'd have slugged her and left her body there in the flat. If anyone had wanted to kill Sophia Atwood, the killer would have made a good job of it.

"As matters now stand, Sophia Atwood is fighting for her life. She's lying in a state of unconsciousness. Someone hit her with a flashlight.

"Now, why use a flashlight and why only one blow?"

"Go on," Drake said. "You evidently have something in mind."

"The reason the flashlight was used as a weapon was because it was the handiest weapon to hand. That means someone was holding the flashlight, making a search of the place when Sophia Atwood caught him or her at it, and the result was the intruder swung the flashlight, a single blow which knocked Sophia Atwood down unconscious and enabled the intruder to escape.

"Therefore the intruder wasn't looking for Sophia Atwood. He was looking for something else.

"Now, if Mrs. Gillman has been abducted, it's because someone wants to come back and search the flat without any possibility of being interrupted. That is, that's a safe assumption.

"Therefore, Paul, someone is searching for something—someone who doesn't know where the object of the search is hidden.

"I'm going to go all out on this case. I want two men on the job at Mrs. Gillman's flat tonight. I want to know if anyone goes to that flat. If anyone should try to search the place, I want to know who it is. I want the license number of the automobile and I want your men to telephone for reinforcements. Then I want to catch the searchers red-handed.

"If anyone should come to Sophia Atwood's house tonight, and I rather think they will, I want to know who it is. And when the prowler gets in, I want your man to telephone for reinforcements, and then you and I are going in and interview him."

"That means four men, to say nothing of reinforcements," Drake said.

"That," Mason agreed, "means four men, to say nothing of reinforcements."

Drake grinned. "It's your party," he pointed out.

Chapter 11

Perry Mason, Paul Drake and Della Street met in the lawyer's office at a few minutes after nine o'clock in the morning.

Both Mason and Drake showed evidences of a relatively sleepless night.

"Well, Paul?" Mason asked, when the detective had settled down with a cup of coffee which Della Street poured from the electric percolator.

Drake shook his head. "Absolutely nothing. I've checked with the men on the job."

"They're still on the job?"

"Not the same men—a new shift went on at five o'clock in the morning. They'll work until one this afternoon, provided you still want to foot the bill."

"I want to foot the bill," Mason said. "I just can't understand why nothing happened."

Mason's phone rang. Della Street answered it, nodded her head to Drake. "It's for you, Paul," she said. "Your office reporting . . . says it's important."

Drake deposited the coffee mug on a newspaper on the corner of Mason's desk, picked up the telephone, said eagerly, "Yes, what is it?"

He was silent for nearly a minute, then he said, slowly and thoughtfully, "Well, I'll be damned."

Again there was a moment of silence; then he said, "No, nothing. Tell them to stay on the job."

Drake hung up the telephone and said, "The blind woman is back on the job."

"Where?"

"At the Gillco Manufacturing Company."

Mason said, "Then it must be Mrs. Bunion. There's only

one blind woman today. How did you find out, Paul? Your men were shadowing the flat, weren't they?"

Drake said, "That's right. Mrs. Bunion came down the front steps from her flat, poking her cane in front of her. A taxicab drove up, the cabdriver jumped out, helped her into the cab, then they drove directly to the Gillco Manufacturing Company."

Mason said, "She came out of the front door of her own flat?"

"That's right."

"She couldn't have," Mason said. "You had men watching the place?"

"We had men watching the place all night," Drake said, "but there's one way she could have done it."

"How?"

"Through the back door."

"But didn't you have a man in the alley watching the back door?"

"After we got back from our visit I put men out," Drake said.

"Now there's no question in my mind but what this blind woman went in her flat, climbed the stairs, walked right on through the flat, went down the backstairs, had someone pick her up and take her out somewhere. Then she came back shortly after we had finished searching the flat but before my second man got on the job watching the alley. She was taken to the back door. She climbed the stairs, went in through the back door, locked it, spent the night in her flat without knowing anything was wrong, and then went out this morning with the taxicab.

"That's the only way it could have happened, Perry. And I just want to warn you that while I'm billing you at cost prices, you're running up altogether too big a bill here. Your client can never pay off and—"

Mason interrupted to say, "I don't expect my client to pay off, Paul. I'm doing this to satisfy my own curiosity. I simply have to know what's back of it all."

"But you've got too many men on the job. You're trying to cover every angle, plug every loophole, and—"

"And in that way we'll get prompt results," Mason said.

"We won't be stringing it out over a long period of time. I'll have a big bill, but I'll know the answer within twenty-four hours."

"I wish I could share your optimism," Drake said. "At least now that we know where Mrs. Bunion lives, you don't need two men on the job at the Gillco Manufacturing Company."

"No," Mason agreed, "I don't think we need more than one man there now, but when she goes to her flat I want two men on the job. I want to find out who it is that comes in the alley and picks her up. It can't be Sophia Atwood now; and in case it's someone who says he is acting for Sophia Atwood, some officious . . ."

"You mean Stuart Baxley?" Drake interposed.

Mason's eyes twinkled. "I *was* thinking of Stuart Baxley."

Drake returned to his coffee, held out the mug to Della Street, who filled it up to the brim with fresh, hot coffee.

Mason sat thoughtfully silent.

Suddenly he said, "I've got it, Paul!"

"Got what?" Drake asked.

Mason grinned. "You and I have set a trap," he said.

"Well?" Drake asked.

"And so far we've caught nothing," Mason said.

Drake nodded.

"Because," Mason said, "we haven't baited the trap. We've just been waiting for something to walk in, and that's no good."

"Not at the rate you're paying private detectives per diem, it isn't good," Drake said. And then after sipping his coffee he asked, "What's the bait, Perry?"

Mason nodded to Della Street. "Take a shorthand notebook, Della," he said. "I'm going to give you some dictation."

Della Street settled herself at her secretarial desk, knees crossed, notebook in front of her, pencil poised.

Mason said, "Della, address this letter to Gerald Atwood at the Hollywood address. Now, look up the date of his death, and I want the letter dated just four days before his death, and I want the letter addressed to him. And start it out: Dear Mr. Atwood."

Drake put down his coffee mug. "What's the idea, Perry?" he asked. "A letter to a dead man?"

"A letter to a dead man," Mason said.

"I don't get it," Drake commented.

"You will," Mason said.

The lawyer turned to Della Street and resumed his dictation.

"In response to your inquiry as to what constitutes a valid handwritten will, I wish to advise that the State of California recognizes a holographic will. This will is one which is entirely written, dated and signed in the handwriting of the testator.

"Such a will requires no witnesses.

"Certain things must be kept in mind, however. First, the will must be entirely in the handwriting of the testator. That means that there must be no other words appearing on the will other than those in the handwriting of the testator. In other words, if you were writing it on a letterhead, tear off the printed matter appearing at the top of the letterhead, particularly any printed material which may have a part of the date connected with it, such as sometimes appears on bank checks where the figures '19' appear followed by a blank.

"Next the document should state that it purports to be a last will and testament. Be sure to provide that all former wills are revoked; that by this will you propose to distribute all of your property. And, as to the person you wish to disinherit, be sure you mention her by name, stating that you intentionally make no provision for her, or that you leave her a nominal sum, such as one dollar or one hundred dollars.

"Then sign the document at the end, and be sure it is all in your *own* handwriting.

"I trust this will answer your inquiry.

"With kindest personal regards. Sincerely yours.

"Now then," Mason said, "type that out, Della, and I'll sign it."

"I still don't get it," Drake said.

"Suppose you're searching for something," Mason said. "What do you do when you find it?"

"You quit searching," Drake said.

"Then suppose something makes you think you haven't found it?"

"Then you start searching all over again," Drake said. "Okay, Perry, I get it now."

Mason said, "If Bernice Atwood got into that Palm Springs house and found a will dated perhaps a year ago, leaving everything to Sophia Atwood, all she had to do was to put that will in a fireplace, be sure it was completely consumed, and that left her sitting pretty. But suppose she thinks that Gerald was going to make a new will entirely in his own handwriting, and that that will was made within a few days of his death; that by that will he revoked all prior wills, disposed of his entire estate and left Bernice out in the cold?"

Drake grinned. "The thing is diabolical in its simplicity. Now then, how are you going to get this letter to her attention without making her suspicious? She already knows that you're interested in the case."

Mason grinned. "I'm going to take a golf lesson," he said.

"A golf lesson?"

Mason nodded. "You've been checking on Bernice," he said. "You say the golf club notified her when Gerald dropped dead. What was the golf club?"

"The Four Palms Country Club," Drake said.

Mason nodded to Della Street. "Ring up the Four Palms Country Club in Palm Springs and ask for the club pro, Della."

Della Street put through the call, then after a few moments nodded to Perry Mason.

Mason picked up the phone. "Hello," he said. "Is this the golf pro at the Four Palms Country Club?"

"That's right," a hearty masculine voice said. "This is Nevin Cortland. May I ask who's talking, please?"

Mason said, without giving his name, "I'm an attorney in Los Angeles, Mr. Cortland. I'm wondering if you are permitted to give golf lessons to persons who are not members of the club.''

"Oh yes. I can give lessons to anyone. If you want to play on the course, you need either a membership or a visitor's card. But under ordinary circumstances, when the course isn't crowded, that can be arranged. You wish to take lessons?''

"I wanted to take one lesson today,'' Mason said. "I am playing in a foursome tomorrow and my swing is way off. I haven't been playing golf for years and I don't want to put up too poor a fight tomorrow. My only consolation is that the other men are just as much out of condition as I am.

"What I want is to get just enough of a lesson so that I will get a little of my touch back. I know that my drives aren't going to be much over seventy-five or a hundred yards on the fly, but that's all I want.''

"That shouldn't be too hard," Cortland said. "What was your name, please?''

"Mason," the lawyer told him. "What time today do you have open?''

"I'm pretty well filled up, but I have time right after four o'clock, only I'm afraid that would be rather awkward for you.''

"That'll be fine," Mason said. "Put me down and I'll be there at five minutes to four. And thank you very much. Good-by.''

The lawyer hung up before Cortland could ask any more questions.

"This I want to see," Drake said. "You swinging a golf club, then bounding blithely over the green to hit the ball again.''

"I'll be good," Mason grinned. "I'll bet I get all of sixty yards on my drives and sink every putt that is under eighteen inches.''

"I'll take the other end of that bet." Drake grinned. "Then what do you expect to do?''

Mason said. "When a man drops dead on a golf course, what happens?''

"I don't know," Drake said thoughtfully. "I've never dropped dead on a golf course.''

"I don't know either," Mason confessed, "but I have an idea."

"What's your idea?"

"Golfers come running out. They try to revive the man. They can't do it. They pick him up and carry him off the course and into the shade. Somebody calls for a doctor. There's probably a doctor on the course somewhere. The word is passed. The doctor comes and checks the man and says, 'This man is dead. Notify the relatives and get the county coroner.'

"There are people playing on the golf course. They don't want to leave a dead man hanging around on the edge of the fairway. Somebody brings a stretcher. They carry him into the clubhouse. Some caddy picks up the man's golf bag and carries it into the clubhouse.

"Now then, the golf bag with the clubs in it is either put in the man's locker, if he has one, or is put in the shop of the golf pro.

"However, after the nearest relative and an undertaker are notified and the coroner has released the body for burial after an investigation, the so-called widow goes out and takes a look through the locker. She particularly goes though the pockets of the clothes in the locker.

"Now, the widow doesn't play golf with a set of men's clubs, nor does she want to continue to pay the rental on a locker at the club."

"Go on," Drake said. "You interest me."

"I thought I would," Mason told him, and then went on. "The widow cleans the things out of the locker. She gives the bag of golf clubs to the pro and tells him to sell them. So Gerald Atwood's golf clubs are probably reposing in the shop of the golf pro at the country club with a price tag on them and an understanding that the pro will get a commission if he sells them."

"I think," Drake said, "from the look in your eye, I'm going to Palm Springs."

"You're going to leave at once for Palm Springs," Mason said. "And you're going to have an operative with you who can pose as a caddy looking for a job."

"And when we get there?" Drake asked.

86

"When you get there, Paul, you're going to plant this letter in Atwood's bag of golf clubs. We'll rumple the letter up and make it look as though Atwood had received it just before he want out on the golf course. He threw the envelope away, folded the letter and pushed it down in the pocket on the side of the bag where a golfer keeps his golf balls."

"I'll be damned," Drake said, and then added after a moment, "You can't get away with it, Perry. There's no way you can let this letter be discovered now without letting Bernice Atwood know it's been planted."

"You want to bet?" Mason asked.

Drake hesitated for a matter of seconds, then answered the question. "No," he said.

Chapter 12

Promptly at five minutes to four Mason presented himself at the Four Palms Country Club, a scenic course running back through a long valley, bordered by the white stucco of luxurious desert homes nestled against slopes which stretched back to shadow-filled mountains.

"I haven't my clubs with me," Mason told the golf pro. "In fact, I haven't played for a long time and I don't know just where my clubs are. I couldn't locate them."

"The woods would have probably dried out," Nevin Cortland said, sizing Mason up with shrewd grey eyes.

"Possibly," Mason said.

"You should play more," Cortland told him. "You need exercise."

"I intend to."

Cortland, medium height, wiry, bronzed, said, "Well, we can fix you up all right, Mr. Mason. You're going out in a game tomorrow?"

Mason grinned. "This is something of a gag," he said. "Some of us who hadn't played golf for a while were talking, and first thing anybody knew there was a foursome fixed up with all sorts of crazy prizes on each hole. I don't want to look like too much of a dub."

"How much playing have you done?"

"Not very much," Mason confessed. "I've been too darn busy."

Cortland said, "I recognize you now from your pictures. You've been in the papers quite a lot."

Mason smiled. "I've had a few spectacular cases."

"Well, let's go out on the practice tee and see what sort of a swing you have," Cortland said.

"I'll want to buy a set of clubs," Mason told him. "I

don't think I'll bother trying to find my old ones, and even if I could find them they'd be in pretty poor shape."

"We can fix that up very nicely," Cortland said, laughing. "Selling new clubs is something I'm always glad to do. You won't have to twist my arm at all, Mr. Mason. Now, let's see, you're tall and have powerful wrists. Let's see."

The pro picked out a couple of drivers from a rack, then a Number Five iron.

"Actually, Mr. Mason," he said, "games are won and lost within fifty to a hundred yards of the green, but I suppose you're more interested in your drive."

"A long ball," Mason said, "will demoralize my opponents, and I'd rather demoralize my opponents than anything I can think of right now."

"I see," Cortland said, leading the way out to the practice tee.

"Let me see you take a couple of swings, Mr. Mason."

Mason obediently swung the driver.

"Try to keep your left arm a little straighter on the backswing. Don't break your wrist quite so quick. Shift your weight on the follow through, but never before. Now, let's try a swing with a ball."

Mason swung and hit the ball.

"Not bad," Cortland said. "Let's try some more. I want to get your swing grooved."

For some twenty minutes the golf pro worked with Mason and then said, "You're coming along nicely, Mr. Mason. I think you'll do all right tomorrow. How would you like to practice your short game a little?"

"I would," Mason said.

They went to the pitch and putting green and Mason put in another twenty minutes.

"That's about enough for today," Cortland said.

"Now, how about clubs?" Mason asked.

"Oh, sure thing," Cortland said. "I've had that in mind. I have a very nice set I can make up for you."

"Do you have any sets that are already matched up and for sale—any secondhand sets?"

"A few of them," Cortland said. "But I'd rather fix you

up with some new clubs that are designed for a man of your height and build, Mr. Mason."

They went into the pro's shop and Cortland picked out a golf bag, went over to the club rack and selected a wood.

"Now, I think this will be just about what you want," he said.

Mason looked at half a dozen well-filled bags which were hanging up on the wall. "What are those?" he asked.

"Oh, some of those are clubs I'm working over," the pro said, "and some of them are for sale."

"How come?" Mason asked.

"Well, one of them, the owner, had a heart attack and has had to give up the game. He could have been playing for years if he'd only followed my advice. But he was a little overweight. He wanted to take off weight fast and he played too hard and too long. Got himself too tired. Now he's had to quit the game for good."

"That nice horsehide bag?" Mason asked.

"That was the property of a man who dropped dead on the court. It was a hot day; he'd been overdoing, working under a terrific strain; and he started out on a morning foursome, finished eighteen holes, stopped and rested at the clubhouse, and then very foolishly went out to play nine more holes on some kind of a bet, so the loser could have a chance to get even. Golf gets blamed for a lot of things, Mr. Mason, that are actually the result of human carelessness, stupidity and downright foolishness."

"How about buying that bag of clubs?" Mason asked.

The golf pro shook his head. "There are a lot of clubs in there you wouldn't need, Mr. Mason, and couldn't use. You should have a couple of woods, four irons and a putter. Any more than that will just confuse you and tend to throw you off your game."

Mason kept his eyes on the golf bag. "How long have you had it?" he asked.

"Not very long. Another man was in here looking at it a short time ago. Thought he might buy it. It's a little more money than he wants to put in it."

"It's for sale?" Mason asked.

"It's for sale, but I haven't a definite price on it at the moment. The widow asked me to see what I could get."

"What do you think it's worth?" Mason asked.

Cortland eyed Mason thoughtfully, finally said, "Just why do you want it, Mr. Mason?"

"If I showed up on the course with that bag," Mason said, "I'd make quite an impression on the others."

"An initial impression, yes," Cortland said. "But I want you to win your game—at least to play the best game you can play."

"Yes, I suppose so," Mason said. "Well, all right, I guess I'll let you fix me up a bag, but that golf bag interests me. Just what generally is the price on it?"

"Just the way the outfit stands," Cortland said. "I think the widow should get a hundred and seventy-five dollars for it."

"Tell you what I'll do," Mason said. "I'll offer a hundred and forty-five dollars, but you'll have to trust me until I can get back to the office and make a check."

"I have no authority to accept any such offer," Cortland said. "Just a minute. I want you to try out this putter. Just take this ball and go out on the putting green and try a few strokes with it. See how you get the rhythm of the thing. Now, Mr Mason, you'll do better if you're keeping pretty well behind the ball. Keep your weight just a little more on your right hip than on your left, and make a smooth, even stroke. Just stroke right through the ball. That putter has a balance that I think will suit you very nicely."

Mason thanked him, took the ball and club and went out on the practice green, was gone for five minutes, returned and said, "I think it works all right. I think I can use this putter nicely."

"I thought you could."

"What about the golf clubs?" Mason asked.

The pro smiled. "I called up the widow. The offer is rejected."

"Well," Mason said, "I want the clubs. I'll go higher. What was the price she said she'd take?"

The pro shook his head. "She's decided not to sell the clubs. She wants to keep them as a memento of her dead husband. He always kept them in his den at home, and she says the room is bare and lonesome without them. She wanted me to bring them to her on my way home tonight. I promised I would."

Mason sighed. "Well, I guess that's that, but I certainly *did* like those clubs."

"You never even had them in your hand," Cortland said.

"I know it," Mason admitted, "but there something about the looks of them—something about the bag."

"It's a nice outfit," Cortland said, and then went on selecting clubs for Mason's bag.

Mason said, "I came away without my checkbook."

"That's all right. We have a lot of blank checks here. You can just fill in one of the blanks and it'll be all right."

"Thanks very much," Mason told him. "I'm going to brush up on my golf game and try to get some exercise."

"That's the stuff," Cortland told him. "But don't overdo it."

Mason filled out a check, took his new golf clubs out to his car, climbed in and drove down the road toward Palm Springs.

At the junction of the main highway Paul Drake, waiting in a car, tapped his horn button twice.

Mason pulled over to the side of the road and stopped.

"How was the golf?" Drake asked.

"Terrible," Mason said. "I creak in the joints. Too much courtroom and not enough exercise. Did you get the letter planted in the golf bag?"

"I did," Drake said, "and I did it very nicely. I went in and got the pro's attention distracted while the young man I had, who is a real golfing enthusiast, just went through everything in the shop."

"Have any trouble getting the right bag?" Mason asked.

"No trouble at all," Drake said. "Gerald Atwood had his name stenciled at the top of the bag. How did you do?"

"I aroused the widow's suspicions," Mason said. "I think I did it artistically enough so she will suspect nothing in the line of a plant, but she now feels certain that I came all the way down here in order to buy her husband's golf bag."

Drake chuckled.

"So," Mason said, "the trap is now baited."

"And we can let some of the operatives go?" Drake asked.

"We'll let everybody go," Mason said. "We've run the blind woman to earth, so that's taken care of, and I don't want to have any detectives waiting around the Hollywood house tonight because that might scare our game away."

"You mean we're going to be watching it ourselves?"

Mason shook his head. "Not watching. We're going to spend the night in the house, Paul."

"Now, wait a minute, wait a minute," Drake protested. "You can't do that."

"Why not?"

"We have no right in there. We . . ."

"Don't be silly," Mason said. "We're representing Katherine Ellis. She has a key to the front door. She has a room there. She has things in the room, and Mrs. Atwood assured me that Miss Ellis or her representatives could come at any time and remove things from the room."

"Remove things from the room, yes," Drake said, "but that's different than staying all night."

Mason grinned reassuringly. "We probably won't have to stay much after midnight, Paul."

"I didn't sleep much last night," Drake protested.

"Neither did I," Mason told him. "Perhaps we can take turns tonight."

"Can we get in all right?" Drake asked.

"Sure," Mason said. "I have Katherine Ellis' key. The authorities have released the premises, and . . ."

"Suppose they have a trap of their own?" Drake asked.

"Then we've baited it for them," Mason said.

Chapter 13

It was well after dark when Perry Mason and Paul Drake parked their cars a couple of blocks from the old-fashioned two-and-a-half-story house and walked quietly down the street.

"Now then," Mason said, holding a latchkey in his hand, "the thing to do is to walk right up to the front door with all the assurance in the world. We fit the latchkey, walk right in and go through the entrance hall, turn to the right at the main stairway, go up the stairway to the first floor, turn to the right—and Katherine Ellis' room is the room looking out on the street. We're going to have to be prepared to sit there, Paul, for a long wait."

"It may not be so long at that," Drake said. "My operative tells me Bernice Atwood came tearing out to the Four Palms Country Club and picked up that golf bag in a hurry. I'll bet terrific odds that as soon as she got home she started going through every bit of the bag."

Mason said, "It won't take her long to make up her mind that she must take some further direct action. We'll assume that in the Palm Springs house she found a will leaving everything to Sophia. She destroyed that will. Now she has reason to believe there's another will, a later holographic will, and that it's concealed in *this* house."

"So we catch her making a search, and what does that prove?" Drake asked.

"It doesn't *prove* anything," Mason said, "but it is evidence looking toward proof.

"After all, Paul, remember that my job is not to get a share of Gerald Atwood's estate for Sophia, but to get Katherine Ellis acquitted of the crime of assault with intent to commit murder.

"What I want to show is that other people were interested in searching this house, and if in the course of their search they encountered a hatbox filled with money, they would be very apt to appropriate the money."

94

"That still doesn't prove Katherine Ellis was innocent of returning later on and socking Aunt Sophia on the bean," Drake said.

Mason chuckled. "You'd be surprised at what some of that evidence will amount to by the time we get it into court. . . . Well, here we are, Paul; right up the walk and then up the steps with all the assurance in the world."

"We should turn on the lights after we get in," Drake said. "Anyone seeing us going in and then not seeing the lights go on——"

"No lights," Mason interrupted. "If we're seen going in by anyone who is really watching the place, we'll be in the soup within the first five minutes."

Mason fitted the latchkey, snapped back the bolt, held the door open. "Come on, Paul."

The house had been closed up and there was a certain stale quality about the air, different from the bracing air of the street outside.

"I guess Aunt Sophia didn't like ventilation too much," Drake said.

Mason said, "You can talk, Paul, until we get upstairs to Katherine's room. Then we're going to sit absolutely quiet without conversation, without any light and without smoking."

"Good Lord," Drake said, "you didn't tell me that!"

"You should have known that," Mason said. "You can't alarm an intruder any more efficiently and thoroughly than by letting him smell fresh tobacco smoke."

"Oh Lord," Drake groaned. "I'll be chewing my fingernails. You really don't need me here, Perry."

"The deuce I don't," Mason said. "I need a witness and I need reinforcements. You have a license to carry a gun. Do you have it?"

"Sure, I've got it," Drake said. "Couldn't I go in a closet and smoke?"

"Smoking is out," Mason said. "Perhaps we won't have to wait very long."

"Perhaps," Drake said lugubriously, "also that officious neighbor who was watching Katherine Ellis come in in the taxicab may have seen us go in and will notify the police. Then we won't have to wait at all. We'll be telling our story to the desk sergeant."

"Police aren't going to take us in," Mason said. "We're up here to check on the personal belongings of my client. We had the permission of Sophia Atwood to enter the house. We have the permission of my client to go through her things."

"In the dark?" Drake asked.

"In the dark," Mason said, grinning. "But no one can tell it was in the dark until after they get in. Now watch your step on these stairs, Paul."

The lawyer led the way up the flight of stairs, which made a complete half-turn as the staircase ascended.

The stairs creaked under the combined weight of the two men.

Mason reached the head of the stairs, groped his way down to the door of the room and entered.

Reflected illumination from the street lights gave enough light so they could find their way. Mason sprawled out on the bed. Drake seated himself in an overstuffed chair.

"We've got to watch out or we'll both go to sleep," Drake said.

"Hush," Mason warned.

"There's no need to keep quiet," Drake said. "The way the staircase was creaking we could hear anyone coming up from below long before he could hear us."

"There are back stairs in the house somewhere," Mason said. "Perhaps they don't creak, or if they did we wouldn't hear them. Now let's keep quiet."

"I can only take so much of this," Drake said. "Of course, if I can sleep it'll help."

"Go to sleep then," Mason said, "and quit talking."

The men sat in the warm silence of the bedroom for several minutes, then the bedsprings creaked slightly as Mason shifted his weight and pushed a couple of pillows back of his shoulders.

Drake shifted his position in the chair almost noiselessly.

The men waited.

From the through street a couple of blocks away the noises of traffic sounded faintly. As temperatures began to change in the house, there were faint creakings.

Drake sighed deeply. There was silence for several minutes, then the deeper rhythmic breathing of the detective indicated he was asleep.

Mason, trying to keep in one position, fought against drowsiness.

The door of Katherine Ellis' bedroom leading to the corridor was propped wide open so that the two men could see the faintest wisp of light in case any intruder used a flashlight.

An hour passed.

Drake's breathing became deeper, turned into a light snore.

Mason noiselessly eased himself along the bed, tapped Drake on the knee.

The detective awoke with a start. "Huh?" he said.

"Sh-h-h-h," Mason cautioned.

The men were silent.

From somewhere on the second floor there sounded a peculiar sliding noise, a noise which came almost as a rhythm of successive sounds.

Mason rose quietly from the bed, pinched Drake's knee.

Drake squeezed Mason's shoulder in order to let him know that he was awake and had been listening.

The two men stood poised, listening intently.

Suddenly there was a reverberating crash—the sound of breaking glass. A man's voice shouted an imprecation and simultaneously a beam of light shot down the corridor, then heavy footsteps running toward the front steps.

"Come on, Paul," Mason said, dashing out into the small hallway which ran along the top of the staircase to intersect the main hallway.

The lawyer was in time to make a crashing football tackle which brought down the figure that was running toward the front steps with a flashlight clutched in its right hand.

The man twisted underneath Mason's body, grasped the flashlight and started clubbing at Mason's head.

The lawyer groped for the man's wrist, slammed the arm back down on the floor. "Lie still," he said, "or I'll choke you. Paul, see if you can find the light switch."

"I'm looking," Drake said.

"Take his flashlight," Mason said, "and you can find a light switch."

"I've got it now," Drake said, and snapped on the light.

Mason partially released his hold to look at the man on the floor.

"Well, I'll be damned," he said. "It's Stuart Baxley, the friend of the family."

Baxley, his face contorted with hatred said, "You snooping, two-timing . . ."

Mason planted an elbow in the other's diaphragm and the words were abruptly shut off.

The lawyer rose to one knee, began to run his hands over Baxley's figure, felt the lump in the other's hip pocket, pulled out a gun and slid it across the floor toward Paul Drake. "Better keep that for a souvenir, Paul."

"Be sure he hasn't got more than one," Drake said. "Sometimes they have a little derringer planted . . ."

"He's clean," Mason said. "Come on, Baxley, get up."

Baxley groaned, rolled over, got to his hands and knees, then slowly came erect, looking like a trapped animal.

"Don't try it," Mason warned. "There's no place where you can go where a warrant for breaking and entering wouldn't find you.

"How about you?" Baxley sneered.

Mason said, "We're in here for a legitimate purpose, and *we* entered with a key. What about you?"

"No comment," Baxley said.

"What was that you tipped over?" Mason asked. "You . . . Oh-oh, there's water. Take a look, Paul."

Drake opened a door from the corridor and said, "I guess this is Sophia Atwood's bedroom. There was a water cooler. It's been tipped over and the big water bottle is smashed."

"Well," Mason said, "I think we'll notify the police and let them . . ."

"Now wait a minute," Baxley said. "We don't need the police in this."

"Why not?"

"I was simply trying to collect some evidence."

"Evidence to convict Katherine Ellis?" Mason asked.

"Could have been," Baxley said, "or it might have exonerated her."

"How long had you been here?" Mason asked.

"Not very long."

"How did you get in?"

Baxley started to say something, then said, "Wait a minute. Do we have a deal or not?"

"Not so far," Mason told him. "Keep talking."

Baxley suddenly clamped his lips together. "I'm not doing any more talking. Not until we have a deal and it's definitely understood what the deal is."

Mason said to Drake, "Look around for a telephone, Paul. Telephone the police. We'd probably better get the homicide squad on the job. They're the ones that have been working up the case against Katherine Ellis."

Drake walked down the corridor, looked around, then using the flashlight they had captured from Stuart Baxley, walked down the creaking staircase, switched on lights in the lower floor.

Baxley looked around for some means of escape.

"It isn't going to do any good to break and run," Mason said. "For your information, I wouldn't shoot you—not on the strength of anything we have against you so far—but when the police come I'll tell them about finding you here, and the police will put out an all-points bulletin and pick you up. Furthermore, in this state flight is evidence of guilt, so you're trapped and you may as well recognize the fact."

Baxley started to say something, then changed his mind.

From down on the lower floor they could hear Drake telephoning for the police.

Then the detective hung up the phone, called up the stairs to Mason, "Shall I turn on the porch lights so the police can come in?"

"Sure," Mason said.

He turned to Baxley. "if you'd tell us what you were looking for, it might clarify the atmosphere somewhat and might lay the foundation for a little co-operation."

"What were *you* looking for?" Baxley asked.

"You," Mason said.

"No, you weren't," Baxley said. "And you were slipping around here in your stocking feet. What were you . . . ?"

Suddenly Baxley caught himself. His eyes narrowed. "Hell," he said, "you weren't slipping around here. You . . ."

"Yes?" Mason encouraged. "What were we doing?"

"No comment," Baxley said.

After a few tense but silent minutes there was a pounding

at the front door—then, as Drake opened the door, the sound of voices, steps ascending the stairs.

Stuart Baxley said to Mason, "You've done it now. You've got the fat in the fire."

Mason was silent, thinking, his eyes level with concentration.

The steps came down the corridor. Drake appeared with two policemen.

"What's going on here?" the officer asked.

Mason said, "A prowler."

"This is the Atwood residence?" the officer asked.

"Right," Mason said.

"Sophia Atwood was assaulted here by her neice and is unconscious in the hospital at this moment?" the officer asked.

"Generally correct," Mason said, "except the assault was not by the niece but was by a prowler."

"And," the lawyer went on after a moment's significant pause, "we have captured *a* prowler."

Baxley whirled to Mason. "Why, you damn . . . You can't pin that on me!"

"Pin what on you?" Mason asked.

"The assault."

"I didn't say anything about pinning it on you," Mason said. "I merely remarked that you were a prowler."

"What about you?" Baxley asked.

"You want to interrogate him?" Mason asked the officers. "Or do you want me to?"

One of the officers grinned. "You folks are doing all right. Now let's see, you're Perry Mason, the lawyer."

"That's right."

"And this man?" the officer asked, jerking his thumb to Paul Drake.

Drake, who had been prepared for the question, slipped a leather folder from his pocket, opened it and showed his credentials.

"A private detective," Mason explained, "in my employ."

The officer turned to Baxley.

"My name's Baxley. I'm a friend of the family."

"How long-standing?" Mason asked.

"None of your business."

"What are you doing here?" the officer asked.

"I was looking for evidence."

"Of what?"

"Of a prowler."

"How did you get in?"

"I got in through the back door. There's a spring lock out there that can be activated with a little piece of celluloid, if you know how."

"*We* know how," the officer said, "but *you're* not supposed to."

"Well, it just happens that I do."

The officer said to Mason. "What were you doing here?"

"I'm representing Katherine Ellis."

"She's being held for assault with intent to commit murder?"

"Right."

"All right, I'll ask again, what were you doing here?"

"I was in the room occupied by Miss Ellis. I had reason to believe a prowler would enter the house."

"What gave you that idea?"

"I thought that a prowler would have a reason."

"Such as what?" the officer asked.

Mason met the officer's gaze. "There's a circumstantial evidence case against Katherine Ellis, and, so far, that's all it is—rather a weak case. I thought perhaps that someone would be trying to plant a little evidence."

"Such as what?" the officer asked.

Mason said, "I don't know. Miss Ellis was accused of having stolen a hundred-dollar bill and has a very good suit of defamation of character against this man, Baxley. How do I know that he wasn't prepared to plant some evidence in the house which would implicate Miss Ellis?"

"That," Stuart Baxley said, "is the most absurd——"

"And," Mason interrupted, "he had a revolver on him. I don't know whether he's got a license to carry it."

"Where's the gun?" the officer asked.

"Paul Drake has it."

"You got a license for that gun?" the officer asked Baxley

"No, I haven't. I wasn't carrying it in public. I was only

carrying it here in the house of my friend. I've got a right to protect the household of a friend."

"How did you get the gun here?"

"No comment," Baxley said. "If you want to prove I was carrying a concealed weapon when I came here, you go ahead and prove it."

"You're a little belligerent, considering the position in which you find yourself," the officer said.

"I don't find myself in any position," Baxley said. "And you watch your step or you'll be the one that's finding yourself in a position. This lawyer is noted for unconventional tactics. You're just taking his word for it that he was sitting there in the room where Katherine Ellis had been living. He had no right to be there. But how do you know he wasn't prowling around the house trying to plant evidence which would weaken the case against his client. That's *his* style."

The officer regarded Mason thoughtfully.

Mason smiled disarmingly, said, "Sophia Atwood told me that Katherine Ellis could get the rest of her things at any time. It was Miss Ellis' room where we were waiting. We got in with a key given us by Miss Ellis."

"When did she give it to you?"

"Before she was arrested."

"All right," the officer said, "we're all going down to headquarters. We're going to close the place up. I have an idea Lieutenant Tragg at Homicide will want a guard put out here. Fred, go call in and make a report. See if you can get Lieutenant Tragg personally. I know he'll be interested in the idea of Mason being out here."

Stuart Baxley grinned.

The officer who was in charge hesitated a moment, then said, "Take these three down to the car with you. Put them in the car. I'm going to take a look around the place myself and see if there's any evidence anything's been tampered with."

"You do that," Stuart Baxley said, "and you'll find that lawyer was in here for some reason. Look in the closet where the money was when it was stolen. A hundred-dollar bill taken out of a hatbox. See if you don't find that this lawyer has planted a hundred-dollar bill somewhere in the back of the closet where he'll claim that it fluttered out of the hatbox when a mouse knocked that hatbox off. That's his style."

Mason grinned and said, "That tells the story, officer. Just search this man Baxley and see if he hasn't got a hundred-dollar bill on him that he was planning to plant in the room occupied by Katherine Ellis."

Baxley jerked back a step. "You can't search me," he said. "You haven't got a warrant."

"Keep your eye on his hands," Mason said. "See that he doesn't get rid of a hundred-dollar bill between here and headquarters. Then book him for breaking and entering and you have a right to search him then. You can tell from the way he's acting now that I hit pretty close to home. He's got a hundred-dollar bill on him."

"Is that a crime?" Baxley asked.

Mason said, "It might be evidence of an intent to commit a crime."

"I always carry a hundred-dollar bill," Baxley blustered. "I keep it as an emergency fund in case I happen to run short of ready cash or am called on to make an unexpected trip."

"All right," the officer said, "come on. You're all going down to headquarters, and don't anybody try to ditch anything along the road."

The officers loaded Mason, Drake and Stuart Baxley in the back seat of the prowl car.

Baxley used every argument at his command to effect his release, alternately threatening and pleading, stating that he would be insulted and his reputation damaged beyond repair if he were taken to headquarters.

The officer drove steadily, skillfully, silently, apparently paying no attention to Baxley's words.

At headquarters, the desk sergeant listened to the story of the officers.

"Who telephoned for the police?" he asked.

"I did," Drake said.

"How did you and Mason get in the house?" the officer asked.

"We had a key—a key given to me by my client, who was a tenant in the building," Mason said.

"You have that key with you?"

"Yes, I have."

"Let me take a look at it."

Mason produced the key. The desk sergeant studied it thoughtfully, tapped it on the desk, started to put it into a drawer of the desk.

"I'm sorry," Mason said firmly. "You'll have to give that key back to me."

"Why?"

"My client has possessions in that room. I'm delegated to get them out."

The sergeant hesitated a moment, then returned the key to Mason.

"How did you get in?" he asked Stuart Baxley.

Baxley said, "I have long been suspicious that there were——"

"How did you get *in?*" the sergeant interrupted.

"Through the back door."

"Was it unlocked?"

"Well, not exactly. Let us say the lock was very vulnerable."

"What do you mean 'vulnerable'?"

"Well, it's a spring lock with a slanting latch. You can take a piece of stiff celluloid or plastic, push it against that latch and get in."

Mason said, "I believe Mr. Baxley was the one who got in through the back door and discovered the unconscious form of Sophia Atwood."

Baxley whirled on him angrily. "You keep out of this!" he snapped. "This is no business of yours."

Mason shrugged his shoulders.

"That true?" the desk sergeant asked.

"That's true," Baxley said. "It happens that I was fortunate enough to discover her. If it hadn't been for that discovery, she would have been dead by this time, and Mr. Mason's client would have been facing a murder charge."

"How'd you get in the time you discovered Sophia Atwood?"

"The back door was standing half open."

"No spring lock?"

"There was a spring lock, but it hadn't been engaged."

"If it had been engaged, you could have sprung the lock anyway?"

"I guess I could have. I didn't know it at that time. It wasn't until I looked around and studied the back-door lock that I realized it was vulnerable."

"How did you know this stunt about using a sheet of stiff plastic to work a spring lock?"

"I read it somewhere in a detective story."

The street door opened and Lt. Tragg came bustling in.

"Well, well, well," he said. "What's all this? Some sort of a convention?"

Mason grinned.

The desk sergeant explained the situation briefly. "These three men were all in the Sophia Atwood house. Apparently Mason and his private detective, Drake, got in there first. They got in with a key to the front door and say they were in the room occupied by Katherine Ellis, Mason's client.

"They heard a crash and went out to find the water cooler had been tipped over and found Stuart Baxley in the house. They collared him and telephoned for the police."

"Which side telephoned for the police?" Tragg asked.

"Mason and Drake."

Lt. Tragg turned to Baxley. "What were *you* doing there?" he asked.

"I have a right to be there. I'm representing Mrs. Atwood."

"Got anything to prove it?"

"I have her word."

"Unfortunately she can't give us her side of the story now," Lt. Tragg said. "You'll have to have something in writing."

"Mason doesn't have anything in writing," Baxley blazed.

"The situation is a little different with Mr. Mason," Lt. Tragg said. "Your detective friend, Levering Jordan, says that Mason was authorized to enter the place all right; that Mrs. Atwood visited with him while Mason was in the place and while the secretary, Della Street, was getting things together to take to Miss Ellis.

"Jordan heard Mrs. Atwood say that Katherine Ellis could come back at any time to pick up the balance of her belongings. What Katherine Ellis can do herself she can do through an agent—that is, if it's a reputable agent such as an attorney."

Baxley lapsed into impotent, angry silence.

"Now, what were *you* doing in there?" Lt. Tragg asked. "What were you looking for?"

"Evidence."

"The police have been all through the place."

"I was looking for something the police might have overlooked."

Mason said, "Perhaps he wanted to plant some evidence so it would look as if the police *had* overlooked it."

Tragg regarded Mason, frowning.

"Such as a hundred-dollar bill in some place in Katherine Ellis' bedroom . . . ?"

"No, no, no!" Baxley protested, impatiently and indignantly. "You've got it all backwards."

"What do you mean backwards?" Lt. Tragg asked.

"I wasn't trying to plant any evidence at all."

Tragg regarded Baxley thoughtfully. "You got a hundred-dollar bill in your pocket?" he asked.

"What's that got to do with it?"

"I don't know. I just asked you a question, that's all."

"That's none of your business," Baxley said. "You don't have a search warrant for me."

"You were caught breaking and entering in a residence," Lt. Tragg said. "We can book you on that, and when we book you, you empty your pockets at the desk. Now, I'm going to ask you again, have you got a hundred-dollar bill on you?"

"All right," Baxley said, "I've got a hundred-dollar bill on me."

"Let's look at it."

Baxley took a card case from his pocket, pulled out a crisp one-hundred-dollar bill.

"Where's the rest of your money?" Lt. Tragg asked.

"In a wallet in my coat pocket."

"Let's take a look at it."

Baxley hesitated, then opened a wallet which he took from his inside coat pocket.

Lt. Tragg counted the money. "You've got about forty-seven dollars in bills in there," he said, "and I suppose you've got some loose change in another pocket?"

Baxley plunged a hand into his right-hand side trouser pocket and brought out a small amount of loose change.

"How long have you had that hundred-dollar bill?" Tragg asked.

"I habitually carry a hundred dollars as a reserve in case I should lose my other money or should need some ready cash to meet an extraordinary expense."

"You mean you carry it with you all of the time?"

"Yes."

"How often have you had to use it?"

"As it happens," Baxley said, "I've never had to use it. I carry it as an emergency fund."

"Then you've had this hundred-dollar bill for some time?"

"Yes."

"Where do you bank?" Tragg asked.

"The Seaboard Security."

"All right," Lt. Tragg said. "If your story is true, then you haven't drawn a hundred dollars out of your account recently. But from the looks of that bill I would say that it hadn't been carried too long in that folder. Suppose we just check with the bank and . . ."

"I got *this* hundred-dollar bill out of the bank this morning," Baxley said hastily, "if that's what you're driving at."

"I thought you told me you had it with you all the time."

"*A* hundred-dollar bill—not *this* hundred-dollar bill."

"What did you do with the other one?"

"I—uh—had it changed."

"At your bank?"

"No, not at my bank, at one of the other banks. I wanted some twenty-dollar bills and I got the hundred changed into twenties. Then I went to my bank and cashed a check for a hundred dollars to get this hundred-dollar bill to replace my reserve supply."

"I'd have liked your story a lot better if you had told it that way the first time," Lt. Tragg said thoughtfully.

"You have no right to adopt this attitude with me," Baxley said.

Lt. Tragg whirled suddenly to Mason. "All right,

Mason," he said, "you were playing a hunch of some kind. What was it?"

Mason said, "I'm sorry, Lieutenant, all I can say is that I *was* playing a hunch. Paul Drake and I were watching the house."

"In other words," Tragg said, "you were acting on the assumption that somebody would try to get in the Katherine Ellis room and plant a hundred dollars?"

Drake gave Mason a hurried glance, then averted his eyes.

Mason said, "I'm in a peculiar position in this case, Lieutenant. You have to realize that. I can tell you that I was in the house as a result of authorization by Mrs. Atwood, the owner of the house, and Katherine Ellis, who was the tenant of the room where Drake and I were waiting. I can't tell you specifically what we were waiting for, but you have a trained mind as an investigator, and if you want to put two and two together, there's nothing we can do to stop you."

Tragg grinned and said, "That is a beautiful example of double talk, but you certainly said one thing which is crystal clear, and that is that if I want to put two and two together in my mind, you can't stop me."

Stuart Baxley said indignantly, "He put the first figure two in your mind, and then he put the second figure two in your mind, and the figure four that you arrived at is just the figure Perry Mason wanted you to arrive at."

Lt. Tragg regarded Baxley thoughtfully. "Baxley," he said, "you're in a very vulnerable position in this case. I'm going to let you go home. I'm not going to book you, but you keep out of that house and don't go around jimmying locks."

"I didn't jimmy a lock."

"Well, it depends upon what you call a jimmy. Tehnically, it was breaking and entering."

"I had as much right there as Mason or . . ."

"No, you didn't," Tragg said. "Now, you keep out of that place. Keep away from it! If you're apprehended anywhere around there in the future, you're going to be in serious trouble. And mind you, I'm not giving you any coat of whitewash right now. I'm simply letting you go. You're a businessman and we can get you if we want you. There's no need putting you in a cell and letting you come up in the morning before a magistrate to have charges preferred and bail fixed. It's better to just let your go on your own recognizance."

Tragg turned to Mason and said, "For your further information, Counselor, it looks as if Sophia Atwood is going to live. They performed an emergency operation, drained at least a large part of the blood clot, but there are complications. She hasn't regained consciousness and, when she does, she may have traumatic retrograde amnesia and not be able to recall anything.

"The reason I'm telling you that is because you'll be reading it in the papers anyway, and it means that we're going to proceed immediately against Katherine Ellis with a preliminary hearing. Then if anything happens that there's a turn for the worse, we can always dismiss this complaint and indict her for first-degree murder before a grand jury.

"Pleasant dreams, Counselor."

"And we're free to go now?" Mason asked.

"You're free to go, and I think I might as well tell you also that it wouldn't be particularly wise for you to be snooping around that house. If you want to get things belonging to your client, we'll give you a police escort tomorrow in broad daylight. You can go there with a car and suitcase—or a moving van or whatever you want—and take everything belonging to your client out of the room. At which time the police officer will make an inventory of what you're taking. In the meantime, don't get caught hanging around that house. Evidence can be planted by *anybody*, and I don't need to warn you, Counselor, that planting evidence is a very serious offense. In your case it could lead to complications which might even result in disbarment."

"I wouldn't think of planting evidence," Mason said.

"No," Tragg said, "I don't believe you would. But you might plant something short of evidence, something that would be perhaps bait for a trap."

"What in the world could I use for bait?" Mason asked.

"I don't know," Tragg said thoughtfully, "but I'm doing a lot of thinking. As you told me, you can't keep a person from putting two and two together."

Chapter 14

"Well," Drake said, when they had taken a taxi back to the Atwood house to pick up their own cars, "do we disregard the police warning and still try to keep the trap under surveillance tonight?"

"We do not," Mason said. "The police meant business with that warning. Over and above that, however, the trap is no longer a trap. The police will have a guard out here within the next fifteen minutes—in case they haven't got one on the job already."

"What will they be waiting for?"

"Waiting for one of us to come back. They've warned all of us to stay away. But Lieutenant Tragg isn't satisfied with any of our explanations. He thinks there's something about that building that enters into the picture, and he doesn't know exactly what it is. He proposes to find out. . . . See that car ahead, with the dent on the rear of the right fender, Paul?"

"Uh-huh."

"Well," Mason said, "for your information, when the prowl car drove up to headquarters that car was parked out in front of the police station."

"Oh-oh," Drake said, "it's a sleeper—a car which had a license plate which is meaningless because it hasn't been issued to anyone. Police use those in their undercover work."

"Exactly," Mason said. "I felt that would be the way Lieutenant Tragg would react to the information he's received. Our trap is not going to catch anything tonight. And it's a shame, because we went to so much trouble to plant the bait."

"But she might still walk in," Drake said.

"Not with all the publicity the place has had tonight,"

Mason said. "A prowl car coming up at high speed, three men being taken to headquarters—and by midnight the radio will be carrying news that we were picked up at the scene of the crime, apparently trying to find evidence, and taken to headquarters. However, if Bernice *is* foolish enough to try to get in there tonight, police will have her picked up before she's been in the place ten seconds."

"And so?" Drake asked.

"So," Mason said, "we have our hand forced. We demand an immediate preliminary hearing for Katherine Ellis or demand that the charges be dismissed. We try to get an interview with the blind woman and in the meantime, I go up to my office where Della Street has signed a receipt for the two cartons of material Katherine Ellis had sent to her by truck shipment.

"You'd better tag along up to the office, Paul, while we open those cartons. There just might be something in them that would be of value."

"What did she say was in them?"

"When the crash came," Mason said, "Katherine Ellis had a lot of expensive clothes.

"She sold the fur coats and everything else for which she could get any money—stripped herself down to bare essentials and came out here to live with her Aunt Sophia. She sensed that she'd be living in one bedroom with limited closet space. She cut her wardrobe down. The things she kept were the ones on which she couldn't raise any money.

"She tells me that she brought along some business documents her father had left which she thought might be worth while—some old gold-mining stocks which were reported to be valueless at the time the estate was appraised, and a couple of old family photograph albums and some old letters.

"I told her I wanted an order to get the things out of storage and take a look through them just to see if there was anything in those old papers that will be of any help."

"Think you'll find anything?" Drake asked.

"Probably not. The chances are a thousand to one," Mason said. "But some of those stock certificates that were appraised as having no value are the things I'm interested in. Sometimes some of those highly speculative issues turn out to be bonanzas."

"I can't help you with that stuff," Drake said. "I'll go home and get some shut-eye. I was sitting around waiting for a call all last night."

"I've had a day myself," Mason admitted, "but I want to take an inventory of those stocks."

"You can reach me on the phone any time during the night," Drake told him, "but be sure it's important. I'm bushed."

Mason nodded, said good night, drove to his office where Della Street already had the stock issues laid out in order, with a typed inventory.

Mason looked at the table on which Della Street had arranged the papers and said, "There doesn't seem to be very much for me to do. You seem to have done it already."

"I've made a complete inventory," she said.

"What's the photograph album?" Mason asked.

"Family pictures. Would you like to see your client when she was three years old? Or a picture in the nude at three months? Or you might like to take a look at the family home, which apparently was mortgaged to the hilt, but it certainly was a pretentious place."

Mason thumbed through the album, turned to the more recent pictures.

"This one," Della Street said, "is your client with her expensive sports car—sitting there behind the wheel at indolent ease. I bet it would have come as a shock if some fortuneteller had tapped her on the shoulder and said, 'Exactly six months from the date of this picture, dearie, you'll be waiting tables."

Mason regarded the picture thoughtfully.

"Any pictures of Aunt Sophia?" he asked.

"Oh yes. She appears in several of the family shots, but they're pretty old and the pictures are the typical fuzzy amateur stuff that people take for no good reason and then paste in family photograph albums."

"I thought the family photograph album had gone out of style," Mason said.

"I think her father kept this up," Della Street said, "and he was a pretty good photographer. Most of the pictures in there are sharp and clear, but running all the way through it are pictures taken with a different camera that are fuzzy, poorly exposed, and out of focus. I just have an idea that Katherine Ellis' mother did those pictures, because they're all family pictures—groups and festive occasions such as a party on Katherine's fifteenth birthday, Katherine with two of her high-school chums.''

"What about the clothes?" Mason asked.

"The clothes are neatly packed," Della Street said, "and I don't think we can do anything better than just leave them folded and in these cartons. We'll have to get a place to store them."

Mason nodded. "Attend to it in the morning, Della. I'm dog-tired tonight. And tomorrow we're going to call this blind woman at her unlisted number. We'll call her until we get an answer, and I'm going to have an interview."

"What can she tell us?" Della Street asked.

"She probably can tell us a good deal if she wants to," Mason said. "For instance, what's the idea of keeping a watch on the Gillco Manufacturing Company, and why use a blind woman as a sentry?"

Della Street said, "Perhaps the blind woman is simply to cover up and served as an excuse to enable Sophia Atwood to come there part of the time."

"Then the blind woman should know *why* Sophia Atwood wanted to go there," Mason said. "But I rather suspect there's something else in the wind."

"What?"

"I think that somebody smuggles information out of the Gillco Manufacturing Company's plant and, while pretending to buy pencils, drops a note in the basket which contains the pencils."

"Now *that* would be something," Della Street said. "Do you suppose the blind woman would tell us?"

"It depends on her character and depends on how we can approach her," Mason said. "Sophia Atwood can't talk. Somebody's going to have to talk if we're going to find out the things we need to find out.

"I'll tell you what, Della, we won't disturb Paul Drake tonight, but first thing in the morning we'll get him on the job and we'll run a double in—a ringer."

"A blind woman?"

"A woman who poses as being blind," Mason said. "We'll get one of his female operatives, get her dolled up in a black dress, dark eyeglasses, with a stock of pencils and ballpoint pens—the works.

"We'll put her out there at the Gillco Company, let her sit where the blind woman sits, and . . ."

"And suppose the real blind woman comes along and catches you at it?" Della Street asked.

Mason grinned. "Then we'll have a showdown which should be productive of results."

He toyed for a moment with the possibilities of the thought, then said, "That just *might* be a wonderful way to find out what it's all about. Let the female operative, posing as the blind woman, be there on the grounds when the blind woman shows up in her taxicab, and have a hidden tape recorder taking down all the conversation. I'll bet it would be illuminating.

"I think we're going to try it, Della. And in the meantime we're going to get ready for a preliminary hearing. The more I think of it, the more important I think it is to have that female operative on the job posing as the blind beggar—or pencil seller, whatever you want to call her.

"Paul Drake is going to hate me for this, but get him on the phone. He's just about had time to get in, have a drink, and start unwinding."

Della Street dialed the number of Drake's unlisted telephone, waited for an answer, then nodded to Perry Mason.

Mason picked up the phone, "Hi, Paul," he said.

Drake groaned. "I knew that the phone would ring before I'd been in the place five minutes. I suppose you've got another brainstorm and you'll want everything done all at once. All right, what is it?"

Mason said, "I want to get a phony blind woman, Paul— a female operative who will dress exactly as the blind beggar has been dressing, will go out to the same place, sit down in the same position, and offer pencils and ballpoint pens for sale."

"I don't see what good that's going to do," Drake protested.

114

"It'll do this much good," Mason said. "We'll leave her there until the real blind woman shows up. Your operative will have a small tape recorder hidden under her dress. When the blind woman shows up, she'll turn it on and make a tape recording of the resulting conversation. A good operative should be able to lead the blind woman into making some very revealing statements."

Drake was silent for a moment.

"You get me?" Mason asked.

"I get you," Drake said, "but I can't get the thing done for at least twenty-four, maybe forty-eight hours."

"Why?"

"Use your head, Perry. We've got to get a woman who will fool the employees there at the plant. She's got to be a ringer for the blind woman. Suppose someone at the plant there is talking with her from time to time—someone, perhaps, who has spent some time visiting with her. This woman has got to be *good*.

"I've got to get the female operative; I've got to coach her on the part; I've got to get my men who have been shadowing the blind woman, get them to rehearse her. I'll try and get it done tomorrow so you can have some results the next day."

"The next day," Mason said, "Katherine Ellis is going to have her preliminary examinations."

"Can't you postpone it?"

"Sure, I can postpone it if I want to, but I don't want to. I think that'd be playing into the prosecution's hands by asking for a postponement. They want delay. They're still working on a case. They are all confused by the events that happened tonight."

"Well," Drake said, "I'll do the best I can. I'll start putting out lines, then I'm going to go to bed and go to sleep. I'll try to have a female operative on the job the first thing in the morning, and we'll try to get her fixed up as a spurious blind woman. Heaven knows what may happen! You know the rules. If she's arrested, you pay all the fines."

"I pay all the fines," Mason said. "Have a good night's sleep, Paul."

Drake said querulously, *"Now* you tell me!"

115

Chapter 15

Judge Morton Churchill took his place on the bench, gathered his robes around him, looked down at the group at the bar, said, "This is the case of the People of the State of California versus Katherine Ellis. The charge is assault with a deadly weapon with intent to commit murder. Are the parties ready?"

Hamilton Burger, the District Attorney, arose. "If the Court please," he said, "I am ready for the people. I do wish to state, however, that as the Court is, of course, aware, murder is the unlawful killing of a human being with premeditation or malice aforethought, or in connection with the commission of a felony, and death may take place within one year and a day from the time of the assault. I am simply stating the law, generally, in order to explain our position, which is that we are proceeding against this defendant by means of a complaint. We are having this preliminary hearing on the complaint. We will ask that she be bound over to answer the charge in the Superior Court.

"In the event, however, that before proceedings in this case are complete, Sophia Atwood should die as the result of the blow which was struck by the defendant, we will dismiss this complaint and proceed before the Grand Jury, asking an indictment for murder.

"We are therefore anxious to see that there is no legal jeopardy attaching to the defendant."

"Why not wait until you have a more settled picture of the medical aspects of the case?" Judge Churchill asked.

"There are reasons," Hamilton Burger said. "We want to perpetuate certain matters of evidence. We want to have the defendant in a type of custody from which she cannot be removed by habeas corpus."

"Very well," Judge Chruchill said. "What about the defendant? Is the defendant ready?"

"The defense is ready," Mason said.

"Very well," Judge Churchill said, "Proceed."

"If the Court please," Hamilton Burger said, "as I have stated to the Court, there are certain aspects of evidence in this case which we wish to have perpetuated. Therefore we are calling certain witnesses and examining them in some detail. As for the rest of the case, we will simply rely upon the rule of law which provides that it is only necessary to show that a crime has been committed and that there is reasonable ground to believe the defendant is connected with the perpetration of that crime."

"Very well," Judge Churchill said. "This Court wasn't born yesterday, Mr. District Attorney. I think I appreciate your position. Go ahead and put on your evidence."

"We call Stuart Baxley to the stand," Hamilton Burger said.

Stuart Baxley stepped forward, held up his right hand, was sworn, and took his position on the witness stand.

"Your name is Stuart Baxley?" Hamilton Burger asked.

"Yes."

"You were acquainted with Sophia Atwood and have been acquainted with her for some time last past?"

"Well . . . Yes."

"On the fourth of this month did you have occasion to see her?"

"Yes, sir."

"Where did you see her?"

"The first time I saw her was when I called at her house as a guest. I was invited to dinner."

"Then what happened?"

"There was something of a commotion. Mrs. Atwood felt she had been robbed of a hundred dollars. There was a bit of excitement and the defendant was, I believe, under suspicion."

"And what did you do in relation to that situation?"

"I had a friend, a private detective, Levering Jordan, of the firm of Moffatt and Jordan. I suggested to Mrs. Atwood that I summon him."

117

"And you did so?"

"Yes, sir, with her permission, of course."

"And then what happened?"

"Mr. Jordan asked the defendant if he could take her fingerprints for purposes of comparison."

"Did she consent?"

"Not only did she refuse, but she called Perry Mason who came to the house and instructed the defendant . . ."

"Objection," Mason snapped.

"Sustained."

Hamilton Burger tried a new approach. "Did you have occasion to enter that house after Sophia Atwood had been taken to the hospital?"

"Yes, sir, I felt certain that . . ."

"Objected to," Mason interposed. "The witness can't testify as to his thoughts."

"Sustained."

Hamilton Burger said, "All right, you had some presently undisclosed reason for entering the house. Now what happened *after* you entered the house?"

"I was very careful to use only a very small fountain-pen flashlight and keep the light down on the floor. I climbed the stairs to the second floor. I moved very cautiously and very quietly. I had a feeling that there was something . . ."

"We're not interested in the feelings of the witness, if the Court please," Mason objected.

"Confine yourself to facts," Judge Churchill warned.

"Well," Baxley went on, "I got to the top of the stairs and I was very quiet. I could hear enough movement to know that there was someone else in the place."

"So what did you do?"

"I remained very still and very quiet."

"You say that you heard motion. Did you hear anything else?"

"Just a peculiar slithering sort of sound."

"A sound made by people whispering?"

"No, I don't think it was whispering, but it was a peculiar slithering sound."

"You had no means of knowing at that time that Counsel-for-the-defense Perry Mason and an employee of his, Paul

Drake, were in the building, occupying the room where the defendant had lived?"

"I had no means of knowing that."

"Then what happened?"

"Then there was a terrific crash, and I . . . Well, the thing took me by surprise and I was all keyed up and I was frightened. I started to run and then—well, the crash was between me and the back stairs, up which I had come, and so I turned and ran for the front stairs. And Mason sprang on me and assaulted me."

"By himself?"

"Paul Drake, the private detective, was helping him. And then after they had me completely powerless, Drake went to phone the police."

"I think you may inquire," Hamilton Burger said to Perry Mason.

"When you went to that house," Mason asked, rising and taking a couple of steps toward the witness box for the purpose of emphasizing his questions on cross-examination, "were you carrying a weapon?"

"I was carrying a thirty-eight-caliber revolver."

"Did you have a permit for that revolver?"

"No."

"Then why were you carrying it? You knew it was illegal to have it in your possession."

"I was carrying it because I felt I was going into a position of some danger."

"Danger from whom?"

"I didn't know."

"And you were prepared to shoot anyone whom you encountered?"

"I was prepared to defend my life."

"You thought your life might be in danger?"

"Yes."

"What was there that made you believe your life might be in danger?"

"Sophia Atwood's life had been in danger."

"Do you know why she was assaulted?"

"I have a very good idea, yes."

"You think all of this trouble was over the theft of a hundred-dollar bill?"

"Frankly, no."

"Now, just a minute—just a minute," Hamilton Burger interposed. "The question is objectionable. I didn't offer an objection, but Counsel is asking the witness for his opinion. As Mr. Mason has so aptly pointed out, we're not interested in what a witness thinks; we're interested in the facts. Let the witness confine himself to facts."

"Very well," Mason said. "Now then, Mr. Baxley, you were present when Sophia Atwood *claimed* someone had stolen a hundred-dollar bill from a hatbox in her closet?"

"Yes."

"And you suggested, did you not, that the defendant might well be responsible for the theft?"

"I did not. I asked a few searching questions."

"What do you mean by searching questions?"

"I asked how many people had been in the house, how many people had access to Mrs. Atwood's bedroom, how many people knew that she kept empty hatboxes in the bedroom."

"Empty hatboxes?" Mason asked.

"Yes."

"How many?"

"Heavens, *I* don't know. She said she had put the money in an empty hatbox."

"But you didn't say 'empty hatbox,'" Mason said. "You said 'empty hatboxes'—using the plural."

"Perhaps I did."

"Did you understand there was more than one hatbox?"

"I don't know. I don't think so. She said 'a hatbox.'"

"But *you* said 'hatboxes' in the plural."

"All right, I was talking about 'hatboxes' in the plural."

"When you were propounding those searching questions you have mentioned, you were talking about 'hatboxes,' plural?"

"All right, I said 'hatboxes,' plural."

"And she didn't correct you by pointing out there was only one hatbox?"

"No. Things were pretty tense at the moment, and there was no question but what in her mind——"

"Just a minute—just a minute," Mason interrupted, holding up his hand. "We're not interested in your thoughts, and we're certainly not interested in having you read the mind of Mrs. Atwood and stating what was in her mind at the time. What I'm trying to find out from these questions is what you deliberately put in her mind—the thought which you implanted that the defendant was guilty of the theft."

"I never said I implanted any such thought."

"You may not have said it, but your actions said it," Mason added. "You asked those searching questions as to the people who had been in the house. You didn't ask any searching questions about your own opportunity to have stolen the money."

"Certainly not!"

"Why not?"

"Because as a reputable businessman, as a friend, I was certainly above suspicion—or I would so consider myself."

"But you didn't consider the defendant, as blood relative, as being above suspicion?"

"I simply asked questions."

"Searching questions?"

"Call them that, if you wish."

"You had a revolver in your possession when you last entered that house?"

"Yes."

"Why?"

"To protect myself in case of necessity."

"You knew it was against the law for you to carry that gun?"

"All right, I knew it was against the law."

"You broke into the house."

"I didn't break—I manipulated a lock."

"Legally that constitutes breaking and entry," Mason said.

"All right," Baxley flared, "take it up with my friend, the District Attorney. I've already come clean with him and we understand each other."

"In other words, you've been given immunity for any crime you may have committed in exchange for your testimony."

"It wasn't on a bargaining basis at all. The District Attorney came to the conclusion that my intentions were absolutely above board."

"You had a hundred-dollar bill in your possession."

"Is that a crime?"

"How long had you had that hundred-dollar bill?"

"I don't know."

"Try and think."

"I can't remember when I got it."

"Then your memory is very defective," Mason said, "because I am in a position to show by competent testimony that you went to your bank and asked for a hundred-dollar bill and . . ."

"All right, all right, I had a hundred-dollar bill. It was my money. I had a right to get it. I had a right to go the the bank and get it whenever I wanted."

"Now then," Mason said, "I'm going to ask you if it is not a fact that you went to that house with that hundred-dollar bill in your possession with the intention of planting that hundred-dollar bill in the room which had been occupied by the defendant so that subsequently, when a detailed search of the room was made by police at your instigation, the hundred-dollar bill would be discovered concealed under a mattress or in some place which would indicate a guilty knowledge on the part of the defendant?"

"Absolutely not."

"I submit," Mason said, "that your actions speak louder than your denial. You were tiptoeing into the bedroom, intent upon planting that bill, when you blundered into a water cooler, tipped it over, and made a terrific crash, and then realized that you were not alone in the house. But before you could escape, you came into contact with Paul Drake and with me."

"That is not true, and I didn't upset that water cooler," Baxley said. "You and Drake must have upset that. It was the crash that frightened me and caused me to start running, trying to get to the stairs."

"And you still deny that you intended to plant that hundred-dollar bill in the defendant's room?"

"I do."

"That's all," Mason said contemptuously, turning his back on the witness.

Baxley started to leave the witness stand.

Judge Churchill tapped with his pencil on the bench. "Just a moment, Mr. Baxley," he said. "I want to ask you a few questions. You knew that the defendant was being accused of taking a hundred dollars from a hatbox?"

"Yes."

"And you went to your bank and got a hundred dollars in the form of a hundred-dollar bill, and then, in the dead of night, went to that house and manipulated a lock so you could enter it?"

"If you want to express it that way, yes."

"And you want this Court now to believe that your intentions were entirely innocent?"

"Yes, sir, Your Honor. Yes, sir."

"Well, I don't believe it," Judge Churchill said, "I don't think you're telling the truth. I think you got that hundred dollars for a sinister purpose."

Judge Churchill glowered at the District Attorney. "This is your witness, Mr. District Attorney," he said. "And the Court is going to tell you here and now that I don't believe his testimony."

"I submit it for what it's worth," Hamilton Burger said.

"Well, in my opinion it's worth nothing. The Court feels that there has been an attempt to frame this young woman with a theft. This case fairly reeks with a frame-up, as far as the Court is concerned."

"But, Your Honor, we have other evidence. We propose to show the defendant made a surreptitious visit to the house in the dead of night and at the very time Sophia Atwood was assaulted; we have evidence which will show that her fingerprints were found on the hatbox from which the money was taken; and we can present a very strong circumstantial evidence of theft and an assault with intent to cover up that theft."

"If she stole the money in the early evening," Judge

Churchill asked, "why should she return to assault Sophia Atwood?"

"We admit that we don't have all of the motivation clearly established," Hamilton Burger said.

"Well, I'm not going to preclude you from putting on other evidence, but as far as this witness is concerned, the Court simply doesn't believe his testimony."

Judge Churchill settled back in his chair with an air of cold finality.

Burger hesitated for a moment, apparently debating with himself whether to try to rehabilitate the witness, then decided against it.

"Very well, Mr. Baxley," he said. "I have no questions on redirect."

Baxley suddenly said, "All right, all right, all right! I'll tell the real truth. I went to try to help the defendant—not to hurt her."

Mason whirled to the witness. "And just how did you expect to help her?"

"I intended to take that hundred-dollar bill and plant it— not in the bedroom of the defendant, but in the closet of Sophia Atwood.

"The hatbox had been knocked off the shelf. I intended to suggest that there should be a thorough search of the closet, on the theory that something might have knocked the hatbox off the shelf—perhaps a mouse or a rat—and that the cover came off the box and that the hundred-dollar bill had fluttered into the back of the closet somewhere—perhaps lodging behind a garment or in a shoe.

"I felt that the police had searched the defendant's room but they hadn't thoroughly searched the closet.

"Then when they found the hundred-dollar bill in the closet, they would assume that was the hundred-dollar bill which had fluttered from the hatbox, that there had been no theft at all, and the good name of the defendant would have been cleared."

Mason regarded the witness thoughtfully. "And why were you so anxious to clear the good name of the defendant that you would take a hundred dollars of your own money and deliberately fake this evidence?"

Baxley said, "My reasons are personal and private. But I will state that I knew that if the defendant could establish the fact of her innocence, and the hundred-dollar bill was still missing, then suspicion would be directed against me; and in view of certain plans I had in mind, I simply couldn't afford to come under suspicion. Now then, that's the truth."

Mason stood for several seconds regarding the witness thoughtfully, then he said curtly, "That's all."

Judge Churchill said, "Just a moment. I want to ask the witness why he didn't tell the truth earlier."

"Because I didn't want to admit that I was trying to plant that hundred-dollar bill in the closet."

"You knew that you were under oath when you were called to the witness stand?"

"Certainly."

"You concealed the real facts; you tried to lie about not remembering when you got the hundred-dollar bill; you tried to make it appear your possession of the hundred-dollar bill was incidental; you concealed your motives for entering the house."

"All right, I did a lot of things I shouldn't have done," Baxley said. "But you can't accuse me of trying to frame any evidence against this defendant. I was trying to help get her out of the jam in which she found herself."

"You didn't tell the District Attorney this."

"Certainly not."

Judge Churchill said, "This is a very peculiar case. There are certain aspects of it that I don't like. I don't like them at all.

"I am not going to prejudge the case; I am not going to jump at conclusions before I hear the evidence. But we have here, apparently, a very refined-looking young woman who is accused of crime under circumstances which impress the Court as being highly suspicious.

"The witness is excused. You may call your next witness, Mr. District Attorney. But I would suggest that your prosecution of this case may be premature, to say the least."

"Mr. Mason hasn't explained what *he* was doing in that

house—not to my satifaction," Hamilton Burger said. "If the Court is going to look at suspicious circumstances—"

Judge Churchill interrupted. "I don't care what motivation Mr. Mason may have had for being in that house. We now have the case of a witness for the prosecution who had admitted to concealing facts; to giving us a version of his conduct which was considerably different from the real truth, and who, only under the stress of cross-examination, admitted that he entered that house surreptitiously and at night for the purpose of tampering with the evidence in this case.

"Now, this is a preliminary hearing. The Court is trying to do justice as best it can. I understand this is not a jury trial; but, nevertheless, this Court wasn't born yesterday, Mr. District Attorney, and it is quite apparent that there are backgrounds in this case which are highly suspicious."

Hamilton Burger said, "Under those circumstances I am going to ask the Court for a recess until tomorrow morning, at which time I may have additional evidence and decide to go ahead with the case, or may offer to dismiss the case and await the outcome of the injuries to Sophia Atwood and then proceed against the defendant before the Grand Jury."

"Is there any objection on the part of the defense?" Judge Churchill asked.

"None whatever," Mason said.

"Very well. The Court will continue this matter until ten o'clock tomorrow morning. Court will take a recess, and I would suggest that there be a great deal of investigative work done between now and tomorrow morning, if this case is to go on."

Judge Churchill left the bench and stalked into chambers.

Hamilton Burger turned without a word to Mason and left the courtroom.

Chapter 16

Once clear of the courthouse, Mason turned to Paul Drake, his manner radiating suppressed excitement. "Paul," he said, "did you get it? Did you get it?"

"Get what?" Drake asked.

"The whole picture," Mason said. "Stuart Baxley was telling the truth. He wasn't telling the whole truth, but he was telling a good part of the truth. Now we know what we're dealing with."

"What are we dealing with?" Drake asked.

"Don't you get it? Paul, the water cooler had been moved."

"Had been moved?"

"That's right—had been moved. Mrs. Atwood had that water cooler in her bedroom. She probably was one of those persons who are on a very low sodium diet and was drinking distilled water. There was a water cooler on the lower floor, because I remember seeing it there, and she had a water cooler in her bedroom. And it had been moved."

"How do you know it had been moved?"

"Because the blind woman crashed into it."

"The blind woman?" Drake exclaimed.

"Exactly," Mason said. "We've been a little bit less than alert, Paul. And we've overlooked the obvious.

"Stuart Baxley was trying to take the heat off that house. As long as officers thought there'd been a theft of a hundred-dollar bill, as long as Sophia Atwood was lying at death's door, it was going to be impossible for anyone to move into that house and take over. But if Stuart Baxley could vindicate Katherine Ellis, and then get Katherine Ellis to move back into the house—then he could have been the fair-haired friend of the family. Don't you see it, Paul?"

"I see your enthusiasm and excitement," Drake said. "But what's all this about the blind woman?"

"We're the ones who have been blind," Mason said. "Katherine Ellis told me that the house was haunted, that she could hear ghostly footsteps at night, with no light. And there was someone in that house when you and I were in there—someone other than Stuart Baxley. There were those peculiar sounds, such as might have been made by someone walking in felt slippers."

"In the dark?" Drake asked.

"It's always dark to a blind person," Mason said. "That blind woman knew the inside of the house just as well as she knows the palm of her hand."

Drake's face showed sudden realization of the point Mason was making.

"Well, I'll be damned!" he said.

Mason said, "Hurry, Paul. We're headed down to see what's happened with your operative who's posing as the blind woman."

"Your car or mine?" Drake asked.

"Yours," Mason said. "I want to think."

"Well, you've done a good job of thinking so far," Drake said.

"But we should have known," Mason said. "Lord, it stuck out all over the case. Sophia Atwood and this blind woman were playing some kind of a game in partnership, and the blind woman knows the house and every stick of furniture in it—every place where everything is and . . ."

"Then why would anyone move the water cooler?" Drake asked.

"That's just the point," Mason said. "The water cooler was moved, but Mrs. Atwood didn't have time to move it back. And the person who clubbed Mrs. Atwood with the flashlight didn't know the water cooler had been moved or appreciate the fact that it would have to be returned to the place that it occupied."

"But why move the water cooler in the first place?"

"Because," Mason said, "she wanted to get at the wall in back of the place where the water cooler stood—or wanted to get at the carpet underneath the water cooler."

Drake sighed. "You certainly go all out on these cases, Perry. You start with a worried waitress and you're winding up with something that's way beyond me."

"It's way beyond me at the moment," Mason admitted, "but I think it has to do with the struggle for power at the Gillco Manufacturing Company."

"We'll soon find out," Drake said. "At least we'll find out what my operative knows."

The detective drove his car with skillful manipulation through the traffic out to the manufacturing district and parked the car in front of the Gillco Manufacturing Company.

"My operative is still there," Drake said. "Evidently there's been no clash with the blind woman."

Mason and Drake left the car, walked up to the woman who was seated with bowed head, holding a basket in her lap.

"How much are the pencils?" Mason asked.

"Whatever you want to give," the woman said in a flat, expressionless voice, "starting with ten cents and going as high as you want. The ballpoint pens are a dollar each, and if you want to pay more, that's up to you. Just don't ask me to make change, please."

Drake bent down to examine a pencil.

The woman said in a low voice that was little more than a whisper, "A man came out about fifteen minutes ago and bought a ballpoint pen. And, when he did it, he dropped a slip of paper in the bottom of the basket."

"Can you get that slip of paper for me?" Mason asked.

"Not without exciting suspicion at the moment. There were figures on the sheet of paper, and that's all—just two rows of figures."

Mason said, "We're sending a cab for you. Pick up your bag of pencils, take the cab, and go to Drake's office. Get that paper and have it ready for him."

"You don't want me to wait here any longer?"

"You've done your job here," Mason said. "Just get away now without being discovered by the real blind person."

"I thought you wanted to have me confront her or have her confront me and get a tape recording of . . ."

"No more," Mason said. "We're beginning to get the picture now."

The lawyer nodded to Paul Drake.

Drake ostentatiously put four dollar bills in the basket, removed two ballpoint pens, gravely handed one to Mason.

"My good deed for the day," he said, and then added, "in case anyone is watching."

Mason and Drake walked back to the place where Drake had parked his car. From the nearest telephone booth Drake telephoned for a taxicab to come and pick up the operative who was posing as the blind woman. Then Drake said, "What do we do now?"

"We go to the house and try to find out what was the real reason for moving that water cooler."

"And what if we are caught there?" Drake asked. "You know we've been ordered to keep out of that house."

"We've been so ordered," Mason said, "but I'm representing a client and my client hasn't ordered me to keep out of the house."

"If the police catch us there, it's going to be rough."

"They *may* catch us there," Mason said. "Our only chance now is to work fast, before they realize what we're up to."

"All this is way beyond me," Drake said. "I can follow you part way, but—well, when you come right down to it, it stands to reason that the blind woman was tied up with Sophia Atwood, but what's the reason for it all?"

"Well," Mason said, "we have a proxy fight in the Gillco Manufacturing Company; we have Hubert Deering chummy with Gillman, the president of the company; we have Hubert Deering's mother, Bernice Atwood, sitting tight on all of the property that belonged to Gerald Atwood in his lifetime; and, with that to go on, we can reach a pretty good conclusion—particularly in view of the fact that there's someone in the plant who is in a position to have access to information, keeping the blind woman posted on the current status of the proxy fight."

"You think that's it?" Drake asked.

"Two figures," Mason said, "one over the other."

Some of the lawyer's excitement began to manifest itself in Drake's voice. "Good Lord, Perry, if that's the solution, you're getting pretty close to home plate."

"Let's hope we're in time at the Atwood residence," Mason said.

"Whom are we trying to beat to the punch?"

"Stuart Baxley, for one," Mason said. "Only I don't think it's occurred to Baxley that there's any significance about the water cooler having been moved—and knocked over by whoever was in the house."

"Do we try to enter surreptitiously and . . . ?"

"We park the car right in front of the house," Mason said. "We use my latchkey at the front door and we walk right on in."

"And suppose there's a police guard watching the place?"

"Then we'll have about five or ten minutes at the outside before we're knee-deep in trouble," Mason said.

Chapter 17

As Mason and Drake left the car, Mason said, "I don't see any sign of a police guard here, Paul."

"That doesn't mean there isn't any," Drake said. "It's just that we don't *see* one."

"Well," Mason said with a chuckle, "we had ourselves to blame. We made a trap and baited it and now we're the ones who come walking into it."

"I don't like it," Drake said. "We're violating police instructions."

"Police can't tell me what to do in order to protect a client," Mason said, leading the way up the walk to the porch of the house. He fitted the latchkey, opened the door and entered.

"Hey!" Drake said. "Aren't you going to ring the bell first? Suppose somebody's home and . . . ?"

The lawyer, however, was already climbing the stairs.

Police had not removed the broken water cooler, and the broken glass and crockery were where they had fallen with the soggy carpet bearing mute testimony to the liquid which had saturated it.

"Well, Paul," Mason said, "you can see what happened. The water cooler had been moved. It hadn't been lifted; it had been partially lifted, partially dragged. You can see the tracks along the carpet. Then someone had neglected to put it back and the water cooler stood between these two doors, right where someone entering the room from that door and leaving it by this one would find the water cooler directly in the path."

"Well, there's nothing here," Drake said. "No reason why the water cooler should have been moved."

But Mason was down on his knees, studying the place where the cooler had originally been located. Then he took a penknife from his pocket, slid it along the edge of the carpet, used the blade to give him a purchase on the corner of the carpet, pulled it back.

"There's a regular trap door here, Paul," he said.

Drake bent forward.

Mason inserted the edge of his knife between the cracks in the board, pried gently, and raised a door on cunningly concealed hinges.

"Good Lord," Drake exclaimed, "the place is full of money!"

Mason regarded the receptacle disclosed by the open trap door, the bundles of currency which had been neatly stacked in the hiding place.

"Holy mackerel!" Drake said. "Look at them! Hundred-dollar bills—there must be a fortune here!"

Mason hurriedly returned the trap door to its place, got to his feet, kicked the carpet back over the trap door.

"All right, Paul," he said, "out!"

"What do you mean—out?"

"I mean out!"

"What are we going to do with this money?"

"What *can* we do with it?"

"We've got to report it to the police."

"And then," Mason said, "Bernice comes forward, claims it was part of the estate belonging to her dead husband, Gerald Atwood; she takes possession, and the fat is in the fire."

"But we can't leave it here," Drake said. "Suppose it should be discovered by other people or stolen?"

"We didn't put it here in the first place," Mason said. "Let's hope that Sophia Atwood regains consciousness so we can have a heart-to-heart talk.

"You can see what happened. In some way she managed to salvage a whole chunk of property in the form of cash, or she reduced it to cash. Bernice moved in and took everything that wasn't nailed down, but Sophia didn't have anything to worry about. She had a comfortable fortune stashed away.

"However, Sophia didn't dare let Bernice get the faintest inkling that she had this concealed fortune, so she acted as a woman who had lost just about everything in the world.

133

"Now then, we're in a predicament, Paul. If she should die without regaining consciousness, we're in a spot."

"And if she regains consciousness?" Drake asked.

"If she does, and can talk, and I can have a confidential conversation with her—well," Mason said, grinning, "we're in a spot anyway, Paul."

"That's the worst of your cases. You always get in some kind of a mess and drag me in with you. If this cache is discovered and looted . . . Good heavens, you've baited such a trap that Bernice is going to come to this house and start searching with a fine-toothed comb and . . ."

"And don't forget our friend, Stuart Baxley," Mason said.

"Well," Drake pointed out, "if they find the money and go South with it—then what?"

Mason said, "We've got to handle things in such a way that the police keep a guard on this house until there's a change, either for the better or for the worse, in Sophia Atwood's condition."

"And in the meantime?" Drake asked.

"In the meantime," Mason said, "we've got to get out of here—fast!"

The lawyer watched his step carefully, picking his way around the broken glass and the wet spot in the carpet.

"Watch your step, Paul," he said. "Grinding some of that glass into the carpet would be a giveaway that there had been visitors. And, right at the moment, we don't want to give anything away."

The lawyer stepped over the last piece of glass, went through the door into the hallway, and came to an abrupt halt.

Lt. Tragg and the uniformed policeman were standing motionless in the hallway.

"Well, hello, Lieutenant," Mason said, after a quick intake of his breath. "How long have you been here?"

"Long enough to hear most of the conversation," Lt. Tragg said. "Let's go take an inventory."

"Have a heart," Mason said.

"I have a heart," Lt. Tragg said. "I also have a head. How did you know this money was here?"

"I didn't," Mason said. "I surmised it from the . . ."

"From what?" Tragg asked, as Mason's voice trailed away into silence.

"I think," Mason told him, "we've already given you enough leads on the case."

Lt. Tragg and the officer moved into the room.

"Come on in here," Tragg said to Mason. "You and Drake sit down over there and keep out of this. Let's see what you've found. Let's see, it was a trap door, I believe . . . Ah, here we are!"

Lt. Tragg gave a low whistle as he raised the trap door on its hinges to dsiclose the hiding place and the money.

"All right," Tragg said to the officer, "start piling it on that table. We'll take an inventory right now."

"Don't you want me to telephone for reinforcements?" the officer asked.

"Not right now," Tragg said. "I want you as a witness to my integrity, and I'm going to be a witness to your integrity. We're going to get this money all out of here and counted before anything happens to it and we're each going to be in a position to swear the other wasn't alone with the money for as much as five seconds."

Tragg started shoveling out the bundles of currency, and the officer piled them on the table, stacking them up in a solid oblong.

"Well, that's it," Tragg said at length.

Mason said, "Take a good look, Lieutenant."

"For what?"

"For an envelope or a piece of paper down on the bottom of that receptacle."

"There isn't anything," Tragg said.

"Are you sure there isn't something there?"

"What do you mean by something?"

"I'm looking for a will," Mason said. "It could be just a folded piece of paper, entirely written and dated in the handwriting of the decedent. It could be a more formal will in an envelope."

"Well, there isn't anything else here. It's slick and bare," Tragg said. "And now we've got the job of counting the money. You folks stay right there and check on the count."

"Those are hundred-dollar bills," Mason said. "They're in packages of . . . how many?"

"Fifty to a package," Tragg said, running through one of the packages.

"Of course, we can't be certain that there isn't more than fifty in some packages, or less than fifty in others, but the packages are all labeled fifty. That's five thousand dollars a package. Let's see what we've got here."

Lt. Tragg counted the packages hurriedly and announced the total in an awed voice. "Three hundred thousand dollars in currency. What the hell do you know about that?"

He suddenly whirled to Mason. "And I'll bet *you* know a lot about that," he charged. "That's what you and Drake were looking for. It's what . . ."

Mason said, "If you're asking me for advice, Lieutenant, I'd keep this discovery very, very hush-hush. I'd keep a guard in the house, and I'd wait to see who comes after that money."

Tragg laughed. "You'd like to have me lock the barn door after the horse has been stolen. I know who came after the money. Your client, Katherine Ellis, came after it—for one. She was caught and had to club her aunt over the head in order to make her escape. But she did manage to tell you enough, so that you and Paul Drake made two attempts to get this money. You could have had a very nice attorney fee with this money."

"Accusing me of intending to steal it?" Mason asked.

"Steal it!" Tragg exclaimed. "Hell, no! You were going to *discover* it. You were going to use it to make Stuart Baxley a red herring. You were going to turn it in as an asset of the Sophia Atwood estate. You were going to get Katherine Ellis acquitted. You were going to have her as the sole beneficiary of all this money. You were going to feather her nest and get yourself a nice fee at the same time. And, dammit," Lt. Tragg said ruefully, "I don't have enough evidence at the time even to say that you're wrong. You *may* be on the right trail. I don't know.

"I can, however, tell you one thing," he said. "Under the circumstances you've stuck your neck in a noose. Hamilton Burger can use this as evidence against Katherine

Ellis, claiming that she knew about the money; that she tried to get it; that that furnishes motivation for the crime; and, in view of this discovery, the Court is going to bind her over for trial. You may be able to get her off before a jury. I don't know. But this hasn't done you any good.

"You should have gone to the police right at the start and told them what you knew."

"But I didn't know," Mason said. "I only suspected."

"My office is open twenty-four hours a day," Lt. Tragg said drily. "And now we're going to get headquarters on the line and ask them to send out reinforcements."

"You're going to make this discovery public?"

"When we discover a cash deposit of this size," Lt. Tragg said, "we don't cut any corners. We put our cards on the table face up. Hamilton Burger will know about this within the next twenty minutes. And in the meantime, gentlemen, there's no reason for us to detain you any longer. Your services as bird dogs are very much appreciated. You'll probably be hearing from the District Attorney before the day is out. In the meantime, and at least temporarily, you are free to leave, and that is what I want you to do."

As Mason and Paul Drake were escorted to the head of the stairs by the officers and went slowly down the stairs, Drake turned to Mason. "All right, Perry," he said, "this is your party. What do we do next?"

"I'll tell you what we do next," Mason said, "but I won't tell you until we get out of the house."

After they had left the house and were starting down the walk toward the car, Mason said, "We'll have a blank subpoena issued on behalf of the defense in the case of People versus Katherine Ellis and we'll serve the subpoena on the blind woman. And that is going to be one hell of a job, Paul.

"You're going to have to have operatives watching the front and back of that house. You're going to have to put someone on duty at the Gillco Manufacturing Company, and you're going to have to serve a subpoena on Mrs. Gooding."

"The manager of the flats?" Drake asked in surprise.

"The manager of the flats," Mason said.

"Why her?"

"Because," Mason said, "we've been taken in by a monumental hoax. When we were ringing Mrs. Gillman's doorbell, trying to get in touch with the blind lady, she was telephoning Mrs. Gooding, asking her to find out what it was all about. And when it appeared that we were determined to either get in the blind woman's apartment or make trouble, Mrs. Gooding let the blind woman slip down the back stairs and into her apartment while we went up and searched the apartment on the second and third floor.

"That whole second-floor flat or apartment is just a big showcase. The blind woman is really living with Mrs. Gooding. By the time we get done we'll find that Mrs. Gooding does the cooking, does the cleaning, and that upstairs apartment is a show place."

"What makes you think so?" Drake asked.

"The place didn't have the feeling of having been lived in," Mason said. "It had a musty, stale atmosphere. What's more, there was no one in the apartment or flat on the third floor. I wouldn't be too surprised if the blind woman doesn't own the whole building and Mrs. Gooding is just a front."

"Well, don't you want to talk with her before you put her on the stand?" Drake asked.

Mason smiled and shook his head. "We're going to have the whole thing come out in court," he said. "When I talk with that woman, she's going to be under oath and she's going to know that any further cover-up will do her no good.

"If I rip the masquerade off and drag her into court, she's going to resent it and the Court will be suspicious. But if I serve a subpoena on her, drag her into court as a witness, and talk with her for the first time in court and she then has to tell the truth, some good may come of it."

"And in the meantime?" Drake asked.

"Oh, in the meantime," Mason said wearily, "Hamilton Burger will let the newspapers in on the secret of the big cache of money. Radio, television and newspapers will blazon the fact that three hundred thousand dollars in cash was found in the house of the woman who was assaulted

138

and is lying at the door of death; that this large sum of cash furnishes the motivation which the police had only suspected but we were unable to prove until brilliant detective work on the part of Lieutenant Tragg of the Homicide Squad brought the secret to light, much to the embarrassment of Perry Mason and a private detective who had plans of their own.''

"And you're going to take a chance on this whole case on what the testimony of the blind woman will be?"

"I'm going to do just that," Mason said. "Sophia Atwood, with a hatbox in her closet full of hundred-dollar bills, a hidden receptacle in the house with packages of hundred-dollar bills; Stuart Baxley, a friend of the family; Bernice Atwood, the legal widow of Gerald Atwood; the fact that the blind woman is at least going under the name of Gillman; the fact that there's a fight on for control of the Gillman Manaufacturing Company; the fact that when Sophia Atwood realized Katherine Ellis had uncovered the hatboxes full of hundred-dollar bills in the closet, she went to all those elaborate pains to lose a single hundred-dollar bill under such circumstances that she could ask the assistance of Stuart Baxley, the fact that Hubert Deering, the son of Bernice Atwood, is pussyfooting around the Gillco Manufacturing Company, and the fact that the blind woman has someone in the company who's feeding out information, and when the blind woman can't be there to get the information, Sophia Atwood would take a turn at selling pencils."

"That pencil-selling was a cloak for industrial espionage?" Drake asked.

Mason nodded.

"But why couldn't whoever was giving the information to the blind woman simply mail her a letter or call her on the phone?"

"Because he was also getting instructions at the same time he was giving the information," Mason said. "And the blind woman wanted to give her orders in person."

"A *blind* woman giving *orders?*" Drake asked.

"Exactly," Mason said.

Chapter 18

Judge Churchill said, "Am I to understand, Mr. District Attorney, there have been rather dramatic developments in connection with this case during the last twenty-four hours?"

"That is right, Your Honor. I would like to put Lieutenant Tragg on the stand."

"Very well."

Tragg took the witness stand, testified to the fact that he and an officer had had a stake-out in the Sophia Atwood house; that they felt the attorney for Katherine Ellis had received information from his client which would cause him to return to the house; that while they had been waiting, Mason and Paul Drake had entered the house, had climbed the stairs, gone to a room where a water cooler had been upset, had found a secret hiding place, and that when Mason and Drake were preparing to leave the officers had confronted them, had taken an inventory of the cash in the hiding place and found that it amounted to three hundred thousand dollars in hundred-dollar bills.

"Cross-examine," Hamilton Burger said.

Mason, in a bored, listless tone, said, "No questions."

Hamilton Burger put on witnesses showing that the flashlight, which had evidently been used as a weapon to club Sophia Atwood, had the unmistakable fingerprints of the defendant.

When he had finished with the fingerprint expert and said, "Cross-examine," Mason asked just one question. "You can't tell *when* those fingerprints were made, can you?" he asked.

"No," the expert admitted. "They could have been made at the time of the assault, or they could have been made sometime previously."

"No further questions," Mason said.

The neighbor testified to the surreptitious midnight visit by the defendant. Again there were no questions on cross-examination.

Hamilton Burger called the taxi driver, who testified to having been called to make the trip to Sophia Atwood's house, had been cautioned against making unnecessary noise.

Judge Churchill from time to time regarded Mason thoughtfully, apparently convinced that the lawyer's attitude of almost bored indifference was due to the fact that Mason had surrendered to the inevitable and considered that the startling developments of the last twenty-four hours would result in an order binding the defendant over.

When Hamilton Burger rested his case, Judge Churchill showed the direction of his thoughts.

"It now appears," he said, "that there is certainly sufficient prima facie evidence to justify an order binding the defendant over. I didn't feel that way yesterday, but the present evidence is . . ."

The judge broke off as Mason rose to his feet and stood, quite apparently waiting for an opportunity to get in a word.

"If the Court please," Mason said. "I desire to put on a defense. I have subpoenaed a witness who is, I believe, totally blind. Her name—or at least the name under which she is going—is Mrs. Gillman. The subpoena has been duly served, and in the event Mrs. Gillman is not here in court, I would like to have a bench warrant issued to bring her in."

A woman on one of the back seats arose and said, "Mrs. Gillman is here in response to the subpoena. I will bring her in."

Mason nodded and reseated himself.

"Well," Judge Churchill said in the silence which followed, "you certainly have a right to put on witnesses for the defense. Of course you understand, Mr. Mason, this is not a case where we usually try the credibility of the various witnesses. The Court takes the testimony of the prosecution at its face value, and if it makes a prima facie case, the defendant is bound over for trial in the Superior Court regardless of any conflicts in testimony."

"I understand," Mason said.

The door at the rear of the courtroom opened and Minerva Gooding entered. On her arm was a woman wearing heavy dark glasses, singularly erect, holding a black-and-white striped cane, walking with a certain assurance and clothed with a regal dignity.

The woman was guided to the witness chair, held up her right hand and was sworn, giving her name as Sophia Gillman.

Mason approached the witness stand. "Mrs. Gillman," he said, "have you ever seen me in your life?"

"I haven't seen anyone for the last ten years," she said.

"Have I ever talked with you?"

"No. I have, however, heard your voice."

"When?"

"When you were talking with Minerva Gooding about me and about getting into my flat and about my connection with Sophia Atwood. I don't know who you found out as much as you did, but I felt then the fat was in the fire."

Hamilton Burger exchanged puzzled glances with Lt. Tragg, then arose and said, "Is this at all pertinent, Your Honor?"

"It's going to be connected up," Mason said.

"Well, I think we should have the connection first," Hamilton Burger said.

"Very well," Mason said, and turned to the blind witness. "What is your relationship to the defendant, Katherine Ellis?" he asked.

"I am her Aunt Sophia," the woman said with dignity.

"What?" Hamilton Burger exclaimed incredulously and then after a moment sat down, all the fight gone out of him.

"And who is the woman who lived in the house and who is known as Sophia Atwood?" Mason asked.

"That was my onetime nurse, Mildred Addie."

"And Mildred Addie impersonated you with your consent?" Mason asked.

"That is correct."

"Would you please tell us the story?"

The witness said wearily, "I guess there's no use trying to hold out anything more now. I am Sophia Ellis Gillman. I had no family except my brother, who was a nice individual but a spendthrift. He worshiped success and had no time to waste on poor relatives.

"The only living soul who took any interest in me was Katherine Ellis. She is, I believe, the defendant in this action. I am sorry I cannot see her.

"Mildred Addie had a rather remarkable resemblance to me in many ways. She worked for me as housekeeper, and then, when I became blind, I had her assume my identity. However, I'm getting ahead of my story."

"Please go on," Mason said.

The courtroom was completely silent, spectators leaning forward to hear better, Judge Churchill regarding the witness in wide-eyed amazement.

"I entirely lost track of my family for some time," the witness went on. "Then I realized I was going blind. In the meantime, however, I had amassed a considerable fortune.

"I didn't want sympathy because of my affliction, or for any other reason, and I didn't care to have my brother, who had asserted his independence as far as a poor relative was concerned, coming honeying around me with any of his wild-eyed promotional schemes.

"I had married Jerome Gillman, who had founded the Gillco Manufacturing Company. He died and left me considerable property. Among the things that he left was a big block of stock in the Gillco Manufacturing Company. He also left a son by another marriage, a worthless, no-good nincompoop—Spencer Gillman, now head of the company.

"It is inconvenient for a blind woman to have a bank account, and it is highly inadvisable for one to let it appear that she has any great amount of worldly wealth. I therefore arranged with Mildred Addie—who was posing as me—to build a place of concealment in the house. From time to time I would visit the place and leave money or securities—mostly money. Because I had lived in the house for years, I knew every foot of it and could walk around at any hour of the day or night with complete assurance.

"Then Mildred—still posing as me—fell in love with Gerald Atwood, a married man who had separated from his

143

wife but who had neglected to go through the formalities of a regular divorce.

"That complicated the situation tremendously. I was forced to write to my brother that I had married Gerald Atwood. I didn't like to do this, but otherwise I would have jeopardized the entire structure.

"Then my brother and his wife were killed in an auto accident, and shortly afterward Gerald Atwood dropped dead on the golf course. Atwood's grasping wife grabbed everything she could get her hands on. Katherine, the defendant in this case, was wiped out financially and left all alone.

"I told Mildred Addie to write Katherine, as Sophia Atwood, and ask her to come and visit. I wanted an opportunity to size up the young woman and to see whether she was a spendthrift like her father or whether she had a good sound basis of common sense.

"I instructed Mildred how to act, and everything was proceeding beautifully until somehow word got around that there was cash being stored in the house. That caused trouble.

"I suppose things would have come to a head anyway, because there was a battle on for proxy control of the Gillco Manufacturing Company. And Spencer, whom I detest—the son of Jerome Gillman by an earlier marriage—knew that his father had left me this stock, that it had been transferred to me and stood in my name, but he didn't know where I was. He began, however, to think that Mildred Addie, who was living as Sophia Atwood, was actually the woman who had his stock.

"By posing as a blind woman, I kept in touch with people in the company who know what a crook Spencer is and want him out of there. But Spencer is smart. He got Stuart Baxley to enter the picture. He was to cultivate Mildred and get the run of the house. I warned Mildred about him, but she wouldn't listen. She was self-willed at times.

"Well, that's what she got for it. She got clubbed over the head."

"Do you," Mason asked, "know who hit her with the flashlight?"

144

"I do not. All I know is it must have been someone who moved that water cooler and left it where I'd upset it. I was never so frightened in all my life. I was moving just as I had always moved, and suddenly I collided with this water cooler and sent it crashing to the floor. Then I heard a man running and men's voices. I had to go down the back stairs and out the back door—which was all right because Minerva Gooding was waiting for me in the alley in her car.

"But as to the night of the assault, I never went near the place. I don't know a thing about it."

"Thank you, Mrs. Gillman," Mason said. "That is all."

The blind woman arose and waited for her escort to pilot her back to her seat.

As she passed the table where Mason was sitting, Katherine Ellis said in a choked voice, "Aunt Sophia!"

"Kit," the woman said, groping her way toward the sound of Katherine Ellis' voice.

The two women embraced.

Judge Churchill waited for a long moment before he tapped gently with his pencil.

"It'll be over shortly," Mason said in a low voice to the blind woman, and then turned to the Court. "If the Court please," he said. "I would like to recall Lieutenant Tragg as my witness."

The Judge, now frankly curious, said, "Lieutenant Tragg to the stand."

"Lieutenant," Mason asked, "did it occur to you that the person who moved that glass water cooler must have left fingerprints all over the glass container?"

"Well, not all over it," Lt. Tragg said. "And I admit that I fell down on the job there at first, but the glass was still in place and we did dust it for latents."

"And did you uncover some latents?"

"We did; a very good set of fingerprints and, moreover, palm prints—undoubtedly the prints of the person who had half lifted, half dragged the water cooler away from the corner where it had been located."

"And did any of the fingerprints you recovered match fingerprints found on the five-cell flashlight which had been apparently used as a weapon?"

145

"Two of three of the prints were the same, yes—but we don't know whose fingerprints they are."

"You do know definitely they are not those of the defendant?"

"Yes, sir."

Mason said, "That's all, Lieutenant. Thank you."

Tragg exchanged a puzzled glance with Hamilton Burger.

Burger started to make some remark to the Court, then, after he had got to his feet, thought better of it and slowly sat down.

Mason said, "My next witness, if the Court please, is going to be a hostile witness. I ask the privilege of asking leading questions."

"Who is this witness?"

"Hubert Deering."

"Very well," Judge Churchill said. "We will reserve ruling on the hostility of the witness until that hostility has been established."

"I notice that Mr. Deering is in court," Mason said. "I would like to have him take the stand."

Hubert Deering, the same lightly built individual whom Mason had encountered at the office of the Gillco Manufacturing Company, arose and strode to the stand, his manner aggressively self-confident. He held up his hand, was sworn, and turned to Mason with animosity apparent on his face.

"You are the son of Bernice Atwood?" Mason asked.

"I am," the witness snapped.

"You are having some business dealings with Spencer Gillman?"

"That is none of your business."

"I am not asking as to the nature of the business in detail," Mason said. "I am simply asking you a question which can be answered 'yes' or 'no' as to whether you have any business dealings with Spencer Gillman or have been having any business negotiations with him."

"That is none of your business."

Mason crossed to the defense table where Della Street handed him a polished metal clipboard containing a sheet of paper.

146

The lawyer, holding the clipboard by its edges, approached the witness stand, extended the clipboard to the witness.

"Attached to this clipboard," he said, "is a carbon copy of a letter to Gerald Atwood about a will. I am going to ask you to study this carbon copy carefully and tell me whether you have ever seen the original letter of which that is a carbon copy."

Mason pushed the metal clipboard into the hands of the witness.

The witness took the metal clipboard, glanced at the carbon copy of the letter, and said, "What's all this got to do with this case?"

"I am asking you," Mason said, "if you ever saw the original letter of which that purports to be a carbon?"

"I understand the question. I'm asking you what that has to do with this case?"

"I'm going to connect it up," Mason said. "Have you seen that letter?"

The witness hesitated, then said defiantly, "All right, I saw that letter. My mother showed it to me. She was all excited about it. I told her it was a plant—something that you had devised as a trap; and I *still* say it's a trap. I don't think you ever knew Gerald Atwood in his lifetime. I don't think you ever gave him any advice. I think this whole thing is a phony."

The witness literally threw the metal clipboard and the letter back at Perry Mason.

Mason said very courteously, "Thank you, Mr. Deering."

He turned and, holding the clipboard by its edges, went to the prosecution's table where Lt. Tragg was sitting with Hamilton Burger.

"Now then, Lieutenant," Mason said, "if you'll develop the latent fingerprints which this witness has left all over the polished surface of this metal clipboard and compare them with the latent fingerprints which you developed on the glass of the water container and with the unidentified fingerprints on the flashlight, I think you'll have a solution to the problem."

Mason walked back to the counsel table and sat down.

It needed but one look at the expression on the face of the witness for Hamilton Burger to get the point and, veteran trial lawyer that he was, he adjusted himself instantaneously to the situation.

"May the Court please," he asked, arising, "this comparison is going to take a little time. May we ask the Court for a half-hour recess?"

"Very well," Judge Churchill said. "Court will recess for thirty minutes."

There was a pandemonium of action in the courtroom, spectators commenting on the dramatic developments.

Hubert Deering pushed his way to the door.

Hamilton Burger cocked an inquisitive eyebrow at Perry Mason.

Mason shook his head. "Flight in this state," he said in a low voice, "is evidence of guilt. The guy's mentality is such that he'll run. He'll start running and keep running. You can pick him up around the Mexican border somewhere and have an even stronger case than we have now."

The blind woman and Katherine Ellis were standing together, talking excitedly in low voices.

Hamilton Burger, looking at them, turned back to Perry Mason.

"Perry," he said, "if you're right on this one, I won't begrudge you the victory."

Mason grinned. "I'm right," he said.

Chapter 19

Judge Churchill returned to court at the end of half an hour.

"Have you finished with the witness Deering?" he asked Perry Mason when court had been reconvened.

"No, I hadn't finished with him, but he doesn't seem to be present. However, Lieutenant Tragg is present, and I would like to ask him a few questions."

Tragg returned to the stand.

"Have you made a comparison of the fingerprints?" Mason asked.

"Yes."

"Did you find a match?"

"I found a series of perfect matches. Hubert Deering left his fingerprints on the flashlight which was used as a weapon, on the glass bottle which held the drinking water."

"Do you know where Mr. Deering is now?" Mason asked.

Lt. Tragg grinned. "I know exactly where he is."

"Where?" Mason asked.

"He left court, went down in the elevator, went to the parking lot, got his car, and started driving south.

"Under my orders, a police plainclothes detective in a plain car with no police markings is following him. That car has a radio-telephone and the officer is making reports to my office here at headquarters and to the offices of various sheriffs along the road.

"Hubert Deering is, at the moment, apparently headed for the Mexican border."

Hamilton Burger arose. "If the Court please, may I make a statement?" he asked.

"Certainly," Judge Churchill said.

"In the last half hour there have been surprising developments.

"The smooth metal surface of that clipboard gave a perfect set of latent fingerprints which are positively identified as those of the same person who left fingerprints on the flashlight and on the water cooler.

"More important, however, is the fact that the woman who is in the hospital as Sophia Atwood, but whose real name apparently is Mildred Addie, has regained consciousness enough to state that her assailant was a man. She saw him briefly before she was clubbed into unconsciousness.

"The doctors do not want her to make any detailed statement at this time, but she is now apparently on the road to recovery. The operation to remove the clot on the brain has been a success."

Judge Churchill frowned thoughtfully. "Have you uncovered motivation?" he asked.

"Apparently," Hamilton Burger said, "Deering, in some way, was made aware that there was a place of concealment in the house. He evidently had reason to believe that shares of stock in the Gillco Manufacturing Company which he wanted to locate had been endorsed to Gerald Atwood and thought the shares were in the possession of Sophia Atwood. He thought he could prove Bernice had the real title if he could find the certificates so endorsed. He felt Sophia had turned these shares of stock as well as all of her other property over to Gerald.

"He was also seeking to find and, if possible, destroy any will which had been made by Gerald Atwood. We are not as yet certain of all of the motivation, but if Deering could have proven that that stock was any part of the Gerald Atwood estate, and his mother could have claimed the stock, there was a handsome bonus to be paid him from the Gillco people."

"Under the circumstances," Judge Churchill said, "it would seem to me that there is only one thing for you to do."

"I do it with good grace," Hamilton Burger said. "I now move the dismissal of the case of the People versus Katherine Ellis."

"So ordered," Judge Churchill said. "Court is going to take a recess, but before I do I'm going to suggest that the witness room be left vacant by all persons except the defendant, her counsel, Mr. Mason's secretary, and the blind woman who has shown herself to be such an interesting figure. I think a family reunion is in order.

"The defendant is released from custody. The case is dismissed. Court's adjourned."

Katherine Ellis, with a glad little cry, placed her hand on Mason's shoulder to give her a boost as she jumped to her feet and fairly flew across the courtroom into the arms of the blind woman.

Mason grinned at Hamilton Burger and took the District Attorney's outstretched hand.

Case after case
Mystery, Suspense and Intrigue...
ERLE STANLEY GARDNER'S
PERRY MASON MYSTERIES

12